CW00661810

GRIMOIRE
ANTHOLOGY

VOLUME II
FALLEN KINGDOMS

TITAN BOOKS

Destiny Universe Created by Bungie

To our community,
You've become the main characters in the stories we tell.
You've filled our worlds with your light and your friendship.
Thank you for your passion for our games and for each other.
Most of all, thank you for playing.

foreword

There is a story behind the story.

At the moment I write this, that story reaches back more than twenty-five years, to *Pathways into Darkness* and an alien god slumbering beneath the Yucatan. It is not a secret plan or a coded revelation, but it is, nonetheless, a tradition: the lore of Bungie's metaverse, a set of motifs that are shared, forgotten, and then reborn, like Guardians, to carry on into new worlds. Whether you grew up haunted by *Marathon*'s terminals and that final image of a bloody hand, whether you chose a side in *Myth*'s war between Light and Dark, or if you've just wondered, in passing, what's going on all with the Bungie sevens—you've seen the hints.

The Grimoire belongs to that tradition. It let a whole new generation of storytellers dive into cryptic arcana and intimate insight that doesn't belong in a traditional cinematic story. Nowhere else could we set up hints to the identity of the Nine in random dialogue in *Destiny*, and then pay them off, years later, in an expansion to Forsaken. There are old puzzles still waiting to be solved—what's with Ghost Fragment: Ghosts, anyway?

But the Grimoire hides another secret tale. It is the story of the people behind the myths, and the web of collaboration, inspiration, and tribute that binds them together. There is not a single word in *Destiny*'s Grimoire, or in the lore books that came after it, that can be called one person's work.

The Fallen are an incredible example of this process. Every word we write about the Fallen is touched by the sound of their language, by their models and animations, and even by the cloth simulation that gives them capes and banners. Not a single story you read in this volume could exist without the work of all those artists and engineers. Even the investment designers, who help make this world worth returning to over and over, shape our imagined relationship to the Fallen by teaching us what we gain when we fight them.

What can a writer add? More meaning, we hope. Something for your brain to chew on after the shooting and the looting. Why are these Fallen here? What do they want? How do they feel about me, and what motivates them to fight on and on when we are so very hard to kill? Maybe their stories will make you feel a scrap of empathy for that Dreg scurrying to obey her Captain's orders. Maybe you start to see yourself in the Fallen. All they want is to survive. So do we. Maybe we'd end up like them, if we suffered the same terrible fall. Maybe there but for the Traveler's grace go we.

This second volume of the Grimoire anthology is a collection of stories that pull on those threads, punctuated by the works of Piotr Jabłoński, Bungie's concept artists, and graphic designers. It captures that deep tension between the Fallen as genocidal raiders and the Fallen as sympathetic hard-times survivors. It asks us whether the chasm of violence and fear between our species is too wide to heal.

So many writers left their indelible mark on this lore, whether directly or through powerful inspiration and collaboration. So many others worked to design, illustrate, and publish it. We owe a very special debt to the localization teams who patiently, tolerantly translate our invented words and alien scripture—none of this could have happened without their monumental efforts.

Above all, we are incredibly grateful to those who collect and study *Destiny*'s lore. You are the reason this book exists, and the reason that more like it can be written. But it also exists because so many people put so much into growing *Destiny*'s world. Take away even one of them, even one hour of their work, and everything would be different.

Remember them.

Seth Dickinson
2019

introduction

They say nothing lasts forever.

That no matter how strong you think you are, there are forces in their own pursuit that won't even regard your effort to steel yourself against oblivion.

That for every great society that has ever risen, another thousand have fallen, swallowed and forgotten by the great maw of time.

But in those shattered remains, new gardens grow, sown across the blood and stories great wars were fought to destroy.

If you look closely—and honor history well enough—you'll see that nothing ever dies… completely.

The energy alters form, the names change, but the story remains the same. The chain is infinite, far beyond our meager comprehension.

There are lessons in every link—they morph into myths, legends, forming a circle where true meaning is too often lost to a claim of righteousness. Then they hold their claim to truth over others, like it was theirs all along.

They offer cautionary tales of how to stand against destruction, processes of how to find alliances among enemies, or teachings of how to balance your existence between two powers that care nothing about claims of any kind.

Whatever they call themselves, or others choose to call them, we are forever one, for better or worse—until a new god rises and another kingdom comes.

From,

A Lightless One,
Forever in Service to the Last Speaker, Who Dared to Speak the Ineffable

Prologue

The Golden Age

The Traveler changed everything. It reshaped our solar system as decisively as it shattered our scientific and philosophical frameworks. To our ancestors it must have been a hammerblow—a glimpse beyond the horizon of expected possibility and into a realm of transcendent power.

The Traveler kindled the Golden Age. But we built it. We remember this with pride, even after so much else has been lost. We settled our solar system and filled it with our work.

Today Cryptarchs and scholars work to distill the legends of the Golden Age into truth. We know that humans lived longer, flew further, and knew more. We know that countless ancient diseases and hatreds were extinguished forever. Human aspiration gives birth to vast engineering projects, sweeping social movements, and even new forms of life.

The Golden Age was not without challenges. Sources speak of internal strife, philosophical rifts—particularly around questions of machine intelligence and 'mind forking'—and enduring scientific enigmas. But humanity and its machine children tackled these problems with pride, vigor, and a contagious sense of pluralist compassion.

Earth

Once our cities lit the whole world.
Now we huddle under the shadow of the
Traveler, in the last place it protects. It is so
very fragile, this small blue ship, our home.

FALLEN KINGDOMS

PART I

PURSUIT

*"Where is the Great Machine? Where is
the Great Machine?"*

—Chelchis, Kell of Stone

CHAPTER 1

The Risen

"When the Ghosts first found us,
those who were chosen were blessed with power,
but not wisdom."

—Lord Saladin

The Dark Age

"No one knew what had happened to the Traveler.
No one understood what had happened to the world.
But they heard the whispered call."

They came from the wild lands, gathering in secret enclaves, slipping through the howling ruins of shattered cities, hoping to find the coast, find a ship, pick up the trail of an impossible dream.

From the deep black came the Awoken, their eyes haunted. Exos marched in the refugee columns, cloaked in moss and shattered memories. And among them came the Ghosts, beginning their search.

It was a time of vast suffering and terrible evil. But there was one hope: the promise of a refuge beneath the Traveler.

Lady Perun

Perun stood at the top of a sloping, narrow path cut into a steep plateau. It was not yet dawn, and the valley below her was foggy and dark.

"Maybe he's not coming." This from a thin woman at Perun's side, the mayor of the crumbling silvery ruins on the plateau behind them.

"We didn't want you wolves here. Lord Segoth knows that."

In answer, Perun pointed into the valley. A red light had appeared.

The mayor let out a wail. "Segoth will kill us all. Or worse, he'll leave us to the Fallen."

Perun shook her head. "Not gonna happen."

The mayor looked at Perun and the two Titans standing on her other side. Then she turned and ran back into the village.

The red lights were larger; already the faint, choppy whine of repaired Pikes filled their ears. "Nine of them," said Saladin.

"Nine, nine hundred, they still gotta come up the pass three at a time." She cracked her knuckles. "Easy pickins."

Radegast looked at her. "The north and south roads are undefended. If they change course—"

"They won't."

"How do you know?"

"It's about making people afraid—of Segoth, and of us. Seeing his goons coming a ways off, knowing he's coming for blood… the dread is part of the punishment. Anyway, he doesn't expect we'll still be here. So he takes the west road, 'cause it's the most visible, and the most direct."

Radegast frowned. "Then it's time to show Segoth that his tyranny will end."

"Not just Segoth," said Perun. She jerked a thumb toward the ruins behind her. Watchful faces poked out of windows and around tarps. "We gotta show them."

The three of them picked up large, rough-hewn metal shields. Behind their shields, each held a worn rifle, wrapped with cloth and chain mail.

The Pike-riders' faces were now visible through early morning gloom. A man in long red robes pulled his Pike ahead as they screeched to a halt.

"Well, well," said Segoth. "The Iron Wolves."

"Cease your insults," Saladin barked.

Perun shot him a surprised look. "That's an insult? I kinda like 'Wolves.'"

"Begone, wolves," Segoth sneered. "These people are mine."

"Wrong," Radegast retorted. "You abuse the powers the Traveler has entrusted us."

Segoth smiled, and shrugged. "Shields up!" Perun shouted.

A hail of bullets slammed into their shields. Perun, Radegast, and Saladin slid backwards on the dusty path. But they dug in their heels, and the shields held.

"Return fire!"

Trapped in the narrow path, Segoth and his warriors fell one by one.

Perun, Radegast, and Saladin reloaded and then Segoth was up again, his glowing Ghost at his shoulder. He fired wildly, and a bullet struck Radegast in the head.

"Got him!" Perun shouted as Radegast collapsed.

"Covering you!" Saladin returned.

Perun, Radegast, and Saladin died many more times than any one of Segoth's men. But any time one of them fell, another would cover them until they staggered to their feet again. The shield wall held. The three gave no ground.

Finally, his robes singed and ragged, Segoth signaled a retreat.

"Iron Wolves!" he shouted as his warriors scattered and a cheer went up from the people in the silver ruins. "I will slaughter everyone who has ever sheltered you!"

In answer, Perun shot him again.

Lord Radegast

Radegast strode through the ashes. A cloud hung in his wake as he made his way to the top of the rise. Scars marred his armor, and his sidearm lay in the dust. He didn't need it, now. The battle was over.

This had been a mining outpost, once. A few buildings and a transport. Nestled amid a small forest, it had been like a precious jewel set atop the dull crown of the wildlands.

Now there was almost nothing left. The warrior began to walk slowly down into the valley. He pulled his helm from his head and let it drop with a muted thud into the ash. Of the forest, only stumps remained. Of the small village there was no trace; the buildings reduced to splinters. Here and there you could see dull gray signs of inhabitation.

At the bottom of the valley, Radegast came to the source of the ash, death, and violence. The Light-bearers were laid out in a row, simple cloth covering their armored and robed forms. There were five of them, and they had been lined up beneath the melted girders of the settlement's great hall.

These warlords had terrorized this part of the wilds for years. Hundreds had died at their hands.

Radegast turned as his companions crossed the valley floor to join him. They had been policing the dead, finding a fitting end for the settlers and miners of the outpost.

Jolder came with a steady glide, energy and fire. Saladin, calm and slow, the weight of the dead on his shoulders. In formation behind them stepped Perun, her boots barely leaving a trace as she walked. They gathered before him.

"Never again." He intoned the words quietly. The others stood as battle-scarred statues.

"We ride against despots and warlords. We hide in these enclaves, hoping that other Light-bearers will not find us. We fear each other." He shook his head, his fists clenched.

"And we should not. We are stronger, together. We are mighty, together. All we have to fear is… this." He pointed down at the dead warlords. "Giving in. Allowing the power of the Light to blind us to what we truly are."

It was Perun, of course, who asked the question. "What are we?" No judgment. No reproach.

Still, Radegast could feel their doubt. He turned upwards, and his eyes settled on the massive span that supported the hall. His eyes shone as he turned back to his fellows.

"We will be what the people need us to be. We will be guardians. We will be protectors. We will hold the last of us together."

His voice rang out across the still valley.

"Our days of hiding are ended. Say it now, each of you. Who among the other bearers do you trust? Who can be counted on to ride with us?"

"Bretomart," said Jolder. "Deidris," said Perun.

"I trust only you, Radegast," said Saladin, and their leader scowled in response. "What are you saying? What are we?" Perun asked again.

Radegast smiled. "We will gather those you trust. We will not wait for this"—he gestured around him—"to force our hand. We will ride against those that would use the Light against our own. Humanity must have protectors. Like the knights of old."

Around them, the dust swirled in the air. Shafts of sunlight coalesced in long slanted bars as the sun dipped towards the horizon.

"Are you with me? Will you stand with me—as Iron Lords?" In the waning light, their answers rang like thunder on the air.

Lord Felwinter

Deep inside a clandestine stronghold sat the dark horse Felwinter and Citan, warlord of the 32nd Sector of Old Russia. A polished obsidian table rested heavily between them.

"Didn't think you'd have the courage to come back here," said the warlord.

"Situational awareness. Not courage. I go where I can do the most good. Thank you for seeing me." Felwinter's voice sounded as hollow as his helmet. Citan wanted to knock it clean off the Iron Lord's bony shoulders. He could do it with a single punch.

"As I recall, you used to have a throne on that Light-forsaken peak, 'til you joined up with the wolves. You're the only warlord I know who held an entire mountain."

"Felwinter Peak."

"No one ever calls it that."

"The Iron Lords do. Though they did ask me to take that throne down."

Citan's laugh shook the room. "How is losing territory ever a good thing for a warlord?" Felwinter folded his hands atop the table. Underneath it, Citan made two fists, a crescent of Light flickering between them.

"Join us and find out," said the Iron Lord. "Turn your sector over to us. You can still patrol it, of course."

Citan's voice lowered. "Of course. You know I'll refuse."

"Then we'll put you down, and take your territory by force. Over and over again if we have to."

"I invite you to my home after you abandon us, and you come to threaten me?" The warlord stood, towering over Felwinter.

"To broker peace." Citan thought that even the voice behind the helmet didn't believe what it said. The floor shuddered as the warlord upended the massive table with one hand. It smashed into the opposite wall, as tendrils of Void Light passed through it and coalesced into Felwinter's leaping form.

Citan had seen this parlor trick before, and judged that he could hammer the Iron Lord out of the air—

But Felwinter's momentum continued into a knee-lift that smashed into Citan's head as the larger man reared back to strike. The warlord fell, the front of his helm shattering. Felwinter landed next to Citan's prone body.

"Lady Jolder taught me that. I can't say the Iron Lords haven't done me any favors," the voice intoned.

"You know we'll burn the world down before we let the Iron Lords rule it," the larger man gasped, breathing out of his mouth, his face a bloody mess. The Void Light in Felwinter's hand snapped—and so did the warlord's neck.

"Radegast is scattered. Perun is indecisive. Silimar wants to build a tower and hide. But they're going to change the world; no one can stop them," Felwinter said quietly to the corpse. He parted his coat and drew a bronze shotgun. "Will it be for the better? I don't know. But they mean to end the fighting, so I don't have to sleep with my back to the wall every night, Light in my hand. And that's not nothing."

He paused, as if waiting for something.

"Normally, this is where I ask you to reconsider. Tell you that you should come with me. See how powerful your Light can become. But I know you, Citan. What you do with the land you take, with its people. The other Lords—especially Saladin— might let you walk away. I'm not going to give them the chance."

Citan's Ghost sparked into view from above, bringing its eye to bear on its fallen charge. The warlord emerged from a radiant column, a frenzied shout at his lips.

Felwinter's shotgun cracked like thunder— once for the warlord, and again for his Ghost.

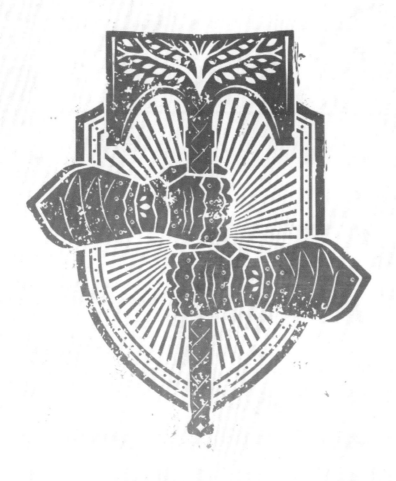

"Only the strong are welcome here."

—Lord Saladin

The Lords' Fall

The struggle. Fighting my brother. Fighting myself. The SIVA ~consume enhance replicate~. A tendril reaches out, crushes my Ghost. I turn to face it. My boots slide in snow thick with blood. If I am gone, then why am I still here?

~SIVA.MEM.??0308

Colovance died by the tanker. Dozens of frames, hundreds, more… he cut them down until he ran out of bullets. Then he smashed them ~consume enhance replicate~. It was not enough.

The same thing that killed Colovance killed me.

~SIVA.MEM.??0309

My axe's flames are almost dead. Even its fire requires fuel.

I need an Urn, but the SIVA has already taken them. The tendrils seek them out, wrap around them, and then ~consume enhance replicate~. More mites swarm out to feed on anything they can touch.

The SIVA learns from what it consumes.

~SIVA.MEM.??0310

Ashraven's cutting her way toward the bunker. Says we should meet her there. She's got an idea—thinks we can hole up in there, maybe get those guns working. Draw off enough of the enemy to give

Jolder's group a shot ~consume enhance replicate~.

It's a bad idea, but it's the best bad idea we have.

~SIVA.MEM.??0311

Finnala always says she doesn't mind dying, because it doesn't last. A few seconds and then the Light comes, bright and warm. And she rises again.

Get up, Finnala! Please get up.

~SIVA.MEM.??0312

We should have been more careful. Should have never contacted the Warmind. Trying to help. Trying to rebuild. Thought ~consume enhance replicate~ was the key.

Feels like we've been fighting for days. Weeks. But we're close. Once we get to the replicator, we ~consume enhance replicate~

Go! I'll hold them off!

~SIVA.MEM.??0313

Felwinter tried to communicate with the Warmind. Called it Rasputin. ~consume enhance replicate~ Said he could make it understand. Tell it we meant no harm.

Rasputin didn't answer with words.

~SIVA.MEM.??0314

I stood at the edge of Lord's Watch and watched the enemy ~consume enhance replicate~.

SIVA curled and thrashed, creating tendrils that lashed out at us. It formed shapes that could grapple us, and angry swarms that buzzed around us before breaking apart to worm their way into every chink of our armor.

Warlords I know how to fight. This is ~consume enhance replicate

~SIVA.MEM.??0315

I don't want to die. I don't want to die. I don't want to die. I don't want... ~consume enhance replicate~

Ghost? Ghost, where are you?

~SIVA.MEM.??0316

This is not my end! I have come too far to die here! I've let one unknown force make me, now ~consume enhance replicate~

~SIVA.MEM.??0409

Saladin: The Iron Lords came together in search of a solution to mankind's struggles. Instead, we found SIVA.

We dreamt of using SIVA to build starships, colonies. We would become what the Traveler always believed we could be.

Ghost: But something happened.

Saladin: SIVA had been lost to time. When Timur tracked it to the Cosmodrome, we thought our quest was finally over. SIVA would be ours for the taking.

Rasputin responded.

More than a hundred Iron Lords entered the Plaguelands. In the end only nine reached the replication chamber. But since we were chosen by the Traveler and our cause was just, we were certain the day would be ours. Until SIVA took control.

It infected our weapons. Our armour. The corruption puppeted us against one another.

In the end, Jolder sealed the chamber with the Iron Lords inside, rather than let SIVA escape. A battle was won. Heroes died. And our mistakes stayed here.

CHAPTER 2

The Fallen

"We have butchers at our gates—
four-armed and eager for slaughter."

The Fallen are ruthless scavengers. Brutal
and uncaring, they arrived on their massive
Ketches in the wake of the Collapse to loot
and pillage our devastated worlds.

There are hints of ancient nobility to the
Fallen—the scars of lost grandeur. The Kells
of their scattered Houses still claim to be
royalty. But they leave only grief and wreckage
in their wake.

Riis

Dreams of Alpha Lupi

This world is rich with family.

You pause to rest. Life is a balm. You must cherish it where you find it.

You do not mean to stay, but longing and kinship forestalls your departure time and time again. These little gardeners are such careful stewards of fragility. They sing songs of disasters averted and loved ones lost. They fashion heavy elements combed from the bones of old stars into objects of peace and beauty.

You must force yourself to be cruel. Your presence is portent.

From Fallen Ground

I am quiet, I am not here, the Fallen cannot see me, they cannot know me.

I am not a shadow, but I move among them, silent, deliberate of motion, and intent as when I entered their hollow one month prior.

I used the light of day to mask my own, because the forest here is barren, it's, it's, it's a dead place, to and fro, a constant buzz as the scavengers go about the business of stripping this world of its old glories. And I watch, I learn, I record and preserve; their every movement is my obsession. I hang on their every word, even though I am not versed in their nightmare tongue, but others are and they will decipher it; they will find the secrets hidden within.

Secrets are like weapons, and I am an instrument of their unmaking. They are enemy, they are cruel, and I will learn and share, and they will be undone.

What is that shouting?

I am deep now, no telling how far in. I have tracked each meter. Mapped every path. But this maze is ever-winding and their cheers now echo, violent with joy, and I hesitate to investigate as I am entering unknown corridors thick with security... Yes, yes, this is a special place, a holy place, a mechanized place, and the shouts merge with screams and the grinding of gears, and the joy joins with pain. There is suffering here, punishment—a, a... a ritual?

I must know so we may know, and I move slow, careful... must... not... be seen... cannot be detected... Meter by meter, anywhere where cover is provided. Quick and with purpose whenever exposed.

I make my way, leaving other avenues unexplored; the cheers must be understood.

But eventually they die. Replaced by the harmony of the pirates' busy days and nights, oh my how they never rest—or rather... when they rest, others continue the work, prepping scavenger sorties, sifting through spoils, readying their fleet, their weapons, their worship. The manner in which they revere machines, I should feel safe here, I should be among their gods... Am I machine? I don't know, I don't know anything. Their worship is not so simple. With the cacophony of excitement no longer echoing, I slow my pace but remain vigilant in my efforts to locate its origin.

It is weeks before I do, weeks before now.

A ceremony has just ended and I am sending out a recollection of what I have seen, because I am seen—these are my final moments, of this I am sure. The ceremony is combat, ritual, and fury, it is a pit and arena where the lesser and unworthy must prove their value or suffer and die. Oh how they fight dirty, oh how they fight to survive—or to thrive. In this pit, before the eyes of an Archon, shamed Eliksni may redeem themselves, lesser pirates may improve their station: a Dreg to a Vandal, a Vandal to a Captain, a Captain to…

This is their forge, their place of judgment, their trial before their betters.

This is what we are up against; kill or die, thrive or perish, they have no use for the weak and they watch and cheer and scream as their Archon looks on.

But I have become careless.

The fervour became a distraction and now the Archon's eyes have found me and I am too deep to run and I think he is smiling…

—The last frantic transmissions of Wren, a brave Ghost of the spectral network

"Tell me more of your Crucible. How you fight each other in the name of the Great Machine."

—Variks, the Loyal

Dreg

"Don't underestimate a cutthroat,
or you'll get your throat cut."

Dregs cling to the lowest rung of Fallen society. Docked of their lower arms in a ritual of humiliation and obedience, Dregs seek to prove their worth. Only a few will survive to gain promotion and regrow their limbs. Their suicidal bravery is fueled by ambition and shame.

Shank

"Death flies on tarnished wings."

Shanks are the bulldogs of the Fallen. Small and tough enough to go where Dregs won't fit, they scout, keep watch, and patrol. Fallen Walkers deploy Shanks from internal bays for tactical support and field repairs.

Vandal

"You could drown the City in the blood they've spilt."

Soldiers, brawlers, assassins, and scouts, Vandals are the seasoned regulars who fill out the skilled roles within a Fallen crew. Whether from distance or up close and personal, they are seasoned, efficient killers, with an arsenal of weaponry and tech to match their bloodlust.

Captain

"Waves of them smashed against our walls, hissing and wailing. But it was the one who stood beyond them, silent and scenting the air, that froze the blood in our veins."

Having clawed and knifed his way to the top, scattering bodies and limbs in his wake, the Captain is the strongest and most ferocious member of the crew he musters around himself. His ration of Ether is the largest, his blades the sharpest, his guns the finest. Upon his shoulders hangs the flag of his House, if he swears loyalty to any. For his crew, the slightest hesitation to comply earns a slash from his sword. Defiance results in immediate amputation, if he is in a good mood, or death, if he is not.

Walker

Fallen Walkers are mobile gun platforms deployed in offensive and defensive roles alike. Though their insect-like design gives them an eerie, almost lifelike quality, these heavily armored monstrosities are purely robotic. Their advanced tracking systems can account for multiple targets as their forward repeaters and massive main gun sweep the battlefield for threats. Mine dispensers provide close defense against dismounted infantry, and an on-board Shank foundry produces armed repair drones.

Walkers are immediate and deadly threats, having ended the Light of countless Guardians. The Fallen do not hesitate to deploy them to provide overwatch for their salvage and extraction crews. Walkers are also commonly used as blocking forces to guard key Fallen assets. At the Battle of Twilight Gap, Walkers engaged in a thunderous artillery duel with the City's gun positions.

The collected wisdom of battle-hardened Guardians suggests Walkers can be beaten by focusing fire on the legs, overloading the Walker and rendering its armored core briefly vulnerable. When the Walker stumbles, Guardians should focus all available firepower on the exposed components beneath the neck plating. Some externally mounted weapons can also be disabled with precise fire.

Servitor

"A floating light, a sleepless eye. Their hope, their faith, their sustenance."

Servitors are living relics of the once-mighty Fallen civilization. Packed with ultra-sophisticated machinery, they process matter and energy into the Ether that the Fallen depend on for life. In battle they support the Fallen with defensive systems and their own powerful energy weapons. Outside, they anchor Fallen comms and provide vital technological acumen.

Servitors have complex relationships with each other and with their Fallen crews.

Servitors are attached to a Prime, a massive Servitor which exists in unclear symbiosis with a Fallen Archon. The Archon conveys the Kell's wishes to the Prime Servitor, and exerts some measure of control. Recent developments suggest that Prime Servitors are more than a focus of worship and logistical activity. They may play a key role in Fallen star flight.

*"Before him, foes will flee or fall. But he will heal
the houses, make them whole."*

—Prophecy, House of Rain

The Great Houses

House of Devils

"The Devils take whatever nature has yet to claim."
—Master Rahool

These are the scourge of the City, the shadow below our walls. This is the House that led the battle at the Twilight Gap, the House we tell our children about to frighten them into behaving.

The House of Devils have now devoted great strength to pillaging the Cosmodrome in Old Russia, hunting for something buried below. If they are not held in check, whatever they find might prove the City's undoing.

—

House of Winter

"Their greed is as much a threat as their blades."
—Commander Zavala

The Fallen House of Winter, led by the ruthless Kell Draksis, have been found operating in and around the Ishtar Sink on Venus. Their interests there seem directed at the ruins of the Academy along the Shattered Coast, but there are concerns that their focus may, in actuality, be directed elsewhere—toward the ominous Citadel that rises like a warning above the Waking Ruins.

House of Kings

"Another great House hides among us…"
—Ikora Rey

The colors of the House of Kings are rarely seen. They act with brutal contempt, as if they hold their rivals—other Fallen and City alike—in disdain. We have yet to grasp the full measure of their strength.

—

House of Exile

"They live among the Hive. Of course they're crazy."
—Cayde-6

There is more than a whiff of desolation about these Fallen. Their ranks are swollen with Dregs; their rags threadbare. Perhaps this is a new House, gathered from the outcast malcontents and disgraced castaways of the others, galvanized by pride or hate or the desire for freedom.

Be watchful. If this is true, they will surely be hungry to secure their position—and that may drive them to bold action.

PART II

RESILIENCE

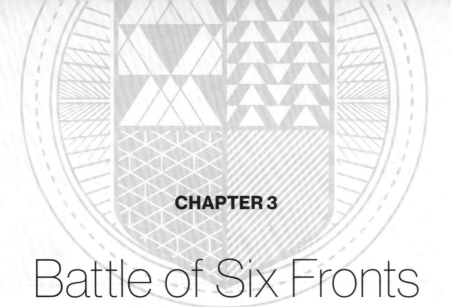

CHAPTER 3

Battle of Six Fronts

At Six Fronts, defending the Wall was not enough. Titans had to become a wall.

It was the City's darkest hour, some Titans broke orders, but the Chain prevailed.

Two Firebreak commanders led a sortie beyond the walls and reclaimed five miles of scorched land from the Fallen.

A zealous few sneer at the legends of Six Fronts. Our invincible defense was a waste they say.

We should have charged.

Onslaught

Verses 60–70

Kell Drifis the Daring declaimed to the dread-makers:

"Whirlwind whisked us to this war-weary world;

We galloped the galaxy to grasp the Great Machine.

It is not our fate to fail on this field!"

And they went, war-whooping for the white orb, to the wall.

Mark the marvelous manslayers who that day marched:

Vililiks the Unvanquished, Vithriks and Vithiliks,

Pirthis and Pithax, called Peerless and Psirris-Slayer,

Rilliks the Revenger and Erivir the Righteous,

But the brutal ones with their bodies barred the way,

The deathless dead ones they call dih-dans.

—

Verses 315–328

Rahdighask reaved ten rikhas into Rilliks's range,

His death-blows drove back the ranks of Dregs,

No numbers could negate the dih-dan's nerve,

Until Kiriviks King-Killer called out to the crew.

Summoning her shock-shooters, the sly Baroness stood

Against Rahdigask at the twelfth rikha and rallied the rabble.

Gunned down again and again, the gruesome dih-dans grew afraid,

And the dih-dans drew back at last, defied and defeated,

And marched no more into the field of the machine-loyal!

Then the righteous righter of wrongs rallied the rabble;

Yes, Kiriviks King-Killer called for a counter-charge!

I wish you could witness the waves of warm-Ethered warbands!

The dih-dans drew ranks, doughty as walls of durmatter,

But Kiriviks carved cracks in their undead configuration!

—

Verses 401–407

Fearful were Kiriviks's Firebreak foes as back they fell.

We thought the white orb, Whirlwind-Maker, we had won!

But alas! Lovely Kiriviks's laughter was not long-lived.

Before the barriers of broad-shouldered dih-dans broke,

She was slain, singing to the sphere, by Osiriks,

The Wirliks who wended his way unwatched through the war-land.

Remember Kiriviks, the righteous who halted ravaging Rahdigask!

—Perinel Fayr's famous alliterative interpretation of an Eliksni war song

Mark of the Six Fronts

Four orders of Titans held six approaches in
the first great battle around the Last City, and
not one front broke.

XXVII   VII-LXI

CHAPTER 4

The Reef Wars

"The Belt is the key to everything."

The Asteroid Belt is a great band of nothingness, speckled with unimaginable wealth. Once a treasure trove for Golden Age industry, the Belt is now a haunted place where Fallen pirates and Awoken patrols skirmish among the whispering carcasses of ancient machines.

Among the asteroids drifts the Reef, lashed together from the ruined ships of an ancient exodus. Here the Queen rules over the Awoken—the farthest known light of civilization.

House of Wolves

"These ones are mine."

—The Queen

The Scatter

Fallen 4

This happens long ago, but not too long to matter.

Ceres rules the Asteroid Belt. Ceres is the white queen of this space, four hundred million kilometers from the Sun. Ceres is round. Round means power, out here: nothing else in the Belt is big enough to crush itself into a sphere with its own gravity. Ceres has its own chemical stars. Shavings of salt and ice that glint in orbit. Like a crown.

There are other lights, newer stars, newer crowns. Warship engines. Another queen is coming to conquer Ceres, because Ceres is full of warrens and shipyards and habitats, because Ceres is round and lucky as a Servitor. Because Ceres is full of the Wolves she wants to rule.

Shark-fierce ships gather in squadrons and tribes. Skiffs. Ketches. The Kell of Wolves has a fleet gathered here. The Kell of Wolves heard the call, and summoned the House of Wolves to prepare for the great battle on Earth. The salvation of the Kell's people depends on their ability to shatter the City. It's a matter of survival.

Now the Wolf fleet turns to meet the Queen.

See the squadrons of Skiffs wrapping themselves in stealth, cold and transparent, knifing out invisible and brave? See the Ketches like broad blades, the bright thoughts of a Servitor guiding them to battle? See them turning, accelerating, waking up their jammers and their arc guns? All doomed. The Kell of Wolves will never make it to the Twilight Gap. The Kell of Wolves put all that strength in one place, and now the Queen of the Reef is coming to break it.

Out there, coming out of the dark, are the Awoken. Not so great a fleet, is it?

Little fighters scattered around like four-pointed thorns. Destroyers and frigates and salvaged hulls pulled out of the Reef. And right at the front, at the speartip, flies the Queen.

The Wolf Kell, practical, brave, tallies strength of metal and equipment. The Kell considers the chance that the Awoken have some secret weapon, something gleaned from hulks in the Reef or whispered up by the witches, and sets that chance aside. The Kell thinks the House of Wolves can win decisively.

So the Kell sends challenge and warning. I AM LORD OF WOLVES, the Kell sends. YOU ARE AN EMPTY THING WITH TWO DEAD SOULS. THIS IS MY HOUSE. THESE ARE

MY TERMS. SURRENDER AND I
WILL ONLY TAKE YOUR SHIPS.

The Awoken fleet cuts their engines.
Drifts. Wolf strike elements, torpedo-
armed Skiffs hidden under jamming and
camouflage, find their firing solutions.

The Queen's ship broadcasts. I AM
NOBLE TOO, she says, OH LORD OF
WOLVES.

The Kell doesn't mind a little banter
before the kill. It gives the Wolf ships
longer to draw the battle away from Ceres.
The Kell replies. YOU HAVE NO LINE.
YOU HAVE NO POWER. Captains and
Barons signal their readiness, Skolas and
Pirsis and Irxis, Drevis, Peekis, Parixas,
all of them bound by fear and loyalty, all
ready for war.

STARLIGHT WAS MY MOTHER.
The Queen's ship whispers in eerie
erratic radio bursts. Servitors begin to
report a strange taste in the void. AND
MY FATHER WAS THE DARK.

Here, at last, too late, the Kell begins to
feel fear. CALL ON THEM, THEN,
the Kell sends, one last mocking signal
before death and ruin, AND SEE
WHAT HELP THEY OFFER.

So the Queen calls, as only she can.
Every Servitor in every Ketch hears it.
Every Captain and Baron roars at their
underlings as sensors go blind, as firing
solutions falter, as reactors stutter and
power systems hum with induction.
Stealth fails. Space warps. The House
of Wolves shouts in spikes of war-code,
maneuvers wild, fires blind.

Behind the Queen's ship, the
Harbingers awaken.

Skolas: Captured

Variks keeps a ragged piece of armor in his pod. It's human tech, Golden Age. Shattered in some ancient battle, pre-Collapse, and left to drift. He found it and he brought it to his quarters so he could sit on it. It's nothing like a throne. Variks doesn't want a throne.

He sits on his ancient shrapnel, unmasked, and whittles at an amethyst with the dead edge of a shock dagger. Music plays (something ancient, pre-Whirlwind, beautiful). The ether in the air is rich and it fills him up with strength. Skolas has been captured, mad Skolas who would have ruined everything. Variks should be happy. He's not. With his little knife and his two arms and his stolen shining thing he feels like a Dreg. He feels ashamed.

He betrayed Skolas twice. At Cybele, and again, now. He will betray Skolas's dream ten times more. Variks will never be strong like Skolas, big like Skolas, a leader like Skolas. Variks will work for the Queen, oversee the Prisons, watch his fellow Fallen (they are Fallen, it's a good name now) fight and die as gladiators who want nothing except a chance to hurt Guardians. Even Skolas.

He tried to use the Vex, word has it. He tried to use their machines. Has that ever worked for anyone? Maybe one. Maybe a few: the Osiris cultists are Variks's favorite people. Maybe that's how you survive this alien star where dead gods slumber and dead heroes walk. You cozy up to powers you barely understand and make yourself useful, or at least inoffensive. You become a parasite, a scavenger, a servant.

That's Dreg strength. That's the strength that keeps Variks alive. It's nothing to be ashamed of.

Abstracts from *The Maraid*

Book VII, Chapter 10

The transmission was broadcasted on all Fallen frequencies. Lacking, at the time, the ability to crack Fallen encryptions, the Master of Crows could discern only that the Fallen Houses were all talking to each other. That was a thing that had never happened before.

Then the Techeuns looked Earthward—and saw the Fallen there becoming bolder. Tactics suggested they were planning a massive attack. We had no interplanetary arrays—no way to warn Earth. We thought we would be able to do nothing but watch.

But then the Wolves arrived from the Jovians. Their army was hundreds of thousands, perhaps millions strong: a dark wave that washed over the Reef, rushing toward the Earth. As soon as we saw them it was clear that if the Wolves reached Earth, the City would fall.

Seemingly oblivious to our existence, the bulk of the Wolf fleet stopped to regroup at Ceres. The Queen's decision was this: attack the House of Wolves, thereby saving Earth but revealing the Reef's presence to any and all enemies in the quadrant; or remain silent, preserving the Reef's invisibility but allowing the City to perish.

Her Harbingers ripped into Ceres, destroying the asteroid and killing Virixas, Kell of Wolves and more than half his House. The remaining Wolves scattered,

burrowing deep into the Belt for cover. There, new claimants to the Kellship quickly arose: Irxis, Wolf Baroness; Parixas, the Howling; and Skolas, the Rabid.

—

Book VIII, Chapter 1

After the Scatter, the frontrunner for the Kellship was Irxis, Wolf Baroness. While Skolas and Parixas scrambled over the Kaliks Servitors, Irxis secured the command of the Orbiks Servitors.

Their history is still unclear, but the Orbiks originate with either another Fallen house—perhaps one that the Wolves absorbed long ago—or a modification of the Kaliks Servitors. Either way, the Orbiks Servitors held permissions on Kaliks Servitors, which allowed Irxis to wreak havoc among her rivals' forces at the start of the Reef Wars.

—

Book VIII, Chapter 2

What Peekis's assault lacked in finesse it made up for in sheer numbers and desperation. Irxis' Ketches were pinned against Eos, and the two sides engaged in the bloody, bitter battle known as the Eos Clash, which left Irxis dead and both fleets nearly decimated. In the aftermath, the Crows salvaged one Orbiks Servitor, Mecher

Orbiks-11, believed to be the last of its programming.

Though technically a victory for Skolas, the Eos Clash came at a terrible cost for him. He docked Peekis's arms and demoted him to Dreg as punishment for his recklessness.

After the Eos Clash, Skolas changed his strategy.

—

Book VIII, Chapter 3

With Skolas and Parixas still fighting, no one expected either to attack the Reef. So by the time Paladin Abra Zire arrived at Amethyst it was too late: the Silent Fang, led by Drevis herself had massacred almost everyone in the station, including Coven Leader Pinar Venj.

Paladin Zire gave chase and followed the Fang to Iris, where, behind the glare of Iris's brightness, a Wolf Ketch lay in wait. But the Ketch was no match for Zire's smaller, faster ships, or her ferocity.

When the Battle of Iris was over, however, it was not Drevis at Zire's feet. It was Parixas.

Grayor, another of Skolas's loyal vassals, had attacked Parixas's Ketch at the same time that Drevis had attacked Amethyst. He, too, had lured Parixas to Iris, then the Silent Fang had used Iris' unusual brightness to disappear just as Zire and Parixas arrived in the system.

Book VIII, Chapter 4

After a string of defeats—at Amethyst, at Hygiea, arguably at Iris—Prince Uldren's Crows finally made headway against the Wolves' encryption. They quickly discovered a seemingly unimportant piece of information: the House of Wolves had incorrectly calculated the eccentricity of the asteroid Bamberga.

So Paladin Imogen Rife chased Drevis, Wolf Baroness, directly into Bamberga's trajectory. Drevis' Ketch was destroyed, and both she and her High Servitor, Kaliks-4, were captured.

It was the first decisive Reef victory since the Scatter. But on her way back to Vesta with her captives, Paladin Rife was attacked at Pallas.

—

Book VIII, Chapter 5

Under Skolas's vassal Pirsis, called Pallas-Bane, the Wolves amassed the largest Wolf fleet that had been seen since the Scatter. The Queen could not use her Harbingers against them—if she did, Imogen Rife and her fleet and all the people of Pallas would have been killed as well.

For years the siege endured. At first, neither side dared to attack the other: on Pallas, Paladin Rife knew that Pirsis had the firepower to destroy the asteroid. Above Pallas, Pirsis held back, hoping to rescue Drevis and Kaliks-4 and the other Wolves that Paladin Rife had captured at the Battle of Bamberga's Wrath. The Queen sought to diffuse the siege by sending Armada Paladins Abra Zire and Kamala Rior into the Hildian Asteroids, where Skolas was rumored to be hiding, but with the help of his tactician Beltrik, the Veiled, Skolas thwarted them.

The stalemate over Pallas was broken by, of all beings, a Dreg. Ironically dubbed Weksis the Meek, the Dreg led dozens of followers in an unsanctioned attack on Pallas. They managed to blast a hole in the Athens Hull, but were stopped soon after by Commander Hallam Fen. Weksis and the surviving followers were imprisoned alongside those they had come to save.

—

Book VIII, Chapter 6

Weksis's attack may have been unsuccessful, but it inspired another, deadlier assault. This time Pirsis, the Bane of Pallas herself led another strike, blasting through the same Athens Hull breach that Weksis had weakened in his assault.

Pirsis's strike team managed to free Kaliks-4, but Paladin Imogen Rife cut them off outside Drevis' cell. Pirsis might have escaped, but she refused to retreat without Drevis. Paladin Rife destroyed Kaliks-4 to prevent the Wolves from recovering it, and, eventually the Wolves were forced back—but not before Pirsis slew Paladin Rife with her own blade.

Finally, Commander Hallam Fen, Imogen Rife's protégé, was able to establish a line of communication with the rest of the Reef. Working with the Techeuns and the Crows, they created an enormous visual illusion of the Harbingers, making it seem as if the Queen had finally decided to cut her losses and destroy the asteroid. It worked—the false Harbingers so scared the Wolf fleet that they broke ranks. Then the combined forces of Commander Fen, Paladin Leona Bryl and Paladin Kamala Rior slammed, capturing Pirsis, Pallas-Bane and driving the rest of the Wolves off.

Hallam Fen brought Drevis to Vesta, years after Imogen Rife had set out to do so. As a reward for his service, the Queen bequeathed him Rife's place among the Seven Paladins.

—

Book VIII, Chapter 7

Finally, Beltrik, the Veiled left the Hildians and massed his fleet at Fortuna, to replenish his Ketches' Ether from the organic compounds found on the asteroid's surface. His ships landed on Fortuna one at a time, the rest forming a defensive screen around its surface. He believed that Paladin Zire would attack the screen and destroy her fleet against the shield wall.

But Abra Zire's fury over the Battle of False Tidings had chilled over the years into an icy, clever resolve. She separated her forces in two, and engaged Beltrik's veil with what he thought was her entire host. But in secret, Abra deployed her second fleet with a weapon the Reef had been working on since Bamberga: Carybdis, a gravity weapon strong enough to knock asteroids off course. Carybdis caught asteroid Tinette in its beam and flung it into Fortuna, destroying both and severely damaging Beltrik's fleet. Beltrik was easily captured in the ensuing chaos, and brought swiftly to the Queen. The fight became known as the Fortuna Plummet, as are, on occasion, the remains of Fortuna and Tinette as well.

After the Fortuna Plummet, one of Prince Uldren's Crows returned with a message from a Fallen, by the name of Variks, of the House of Judgment.

—

Book VIII, Chapter 8

In desperation, Skolas personally led an all-out assault on the military fortress of Cybele. Little did he know that the Queen knew of his plans, thanks to the word of Variks, of the House of Judgment. No sooner had Skolas's Ketches arrived at the asteroid than all four Armada Paladins—Abra Zire, Kamala Rior, Leona Bryl and Hallam Fen—caught him in a pincer movement. Kaliks-12, the High Servitor of Skriviks, the Sharp-Eyed, tried to escape, but Abra Zire chased it down.

Skolas's Cybele Uprising had failed. He, Skriviks, Kaliks-12 and the rest of his leaders were cast into the Queen's prison. The Reef Wars were effectively over.

—

Book VIII, Chapter 9

Variks of the House of Judgment declared Queen Mara Sov the new Kell of Wolves, and advised those captured at Cybele to serve her. The first among these to pledge their loyalty to the Queen was one called Saviks, who was given the honor of serving in the Queen's throne room, to the right of the Queen herself.

[See Book IX, Chapter 3, subsection "The Queenbreakers."]

—

Book VIII, Chapter 10

Though many Wolves knelt to the Queen, some refused to admit the war was over. A group of Wolves rallied under the banner of a new would-be Kell: Veliniks, called the Ravenous.

But before Veliniks could strike at the Reef, the Reef struck at him: Lieutenant Petra Venj, a Corsair who had served under Paladin Abra Zire during the Hildian Campaign, hunted down and captured Veliniks.

The Fortuna Plummet

The Reef 3

SNAP TRAFFIC! 225 RADIAN MIRAGE HALT ALL TRAFFIC. STAND BY FOR SNAP. MESSAGE TO FOLLOW

PUBLIC KEY 080 641 DWS REGAL FROM: PLDN ABRA ZIRE [PLDN CMD TF 4.1] TO: ALL TASK GROUP ELEMENT LEADERS SUBJECT: OPLAN AND FRAGMENT ORDERS

MESSAGE IS:

1. Beltrik the Veiled [HVT R3] and loyal spaceborne elements have been localized to 19 Fortuna. Beltrik is chief Wolf strategist. Corsair recon confirms that HVT R3 ships are resupplying ether and performing high-tempo logistical operations. Recon elements and COLLABINT sources agree that Beltrik will roll one ship at a time into the resupply pocket while holding all other assets to screen.

2. TF 4.1 will attack. Targets are HVT R3 spaceborne assets. Objective is annihilation of spaceborne assets and capture/ nullification of HVT R3. Designate targets VEIL HAND.

2a. Due to history of violence between PLDN CMD TF 4.1 and HVT R3, particularly Battle of False Tidings/Hildian Campaign, Beltrik expects TF 4.1 to engage his screen directly. We will exploit this expectation. Fragment orders follow.

3. PETRA VENJ will detach select warships and air wing elements to form TF 4.2 MASS LENS. TF 4.2 is directed to engage VEIL HAND screen elements with skirmishers. TF 4.2 will deny main battle while pinning down VEIL HAND forces at 19 Fortuna. TF 4.2 will receive missile and torpedo assets to force VEIL HAND into maintaining tight mutual CIWS/ESM support.

3a. Decisive engagement with VEIL HAND in 4.2 MASS LENS AO is forbidden until GO CONTINGENCY satisfied. Prioritize FORCECON.

4. Remaining TF 4.1 will maneuver immediately to rendezvous with 687 Tinette. Tinette is on close approach with 19 Fortuna. TF 4.1 frigates and fighters will perform recon denial against VEIL HAND scouts.

4a. Upon rendezvous with 687 Tinette, TF 4.1 will deploy CARYBDIS. ***This is a CARYBDIS RELEASE (MAJESTY DIRECT)!***. TF 4.1 will maneuver in Tinette's shadow as it retrajectorizes for intercept.

5. GO CONTINGENCY: Upon collision of 687 Tinette and 19 Fortuna TF 4.1 and TF 4.2 will IMMEDIATELY close for decisive engagement. VEIL HAND

C4I will be critically degraded and all targets will be maneuvering away from mutual support. Skirmishers and air wing will provide TARCAP and destroy VEIL HAND light warships as they attempt to reform. EWAR assets will isolate hostile heavy warships from C4I and spoof bad datalinks. Main combatants will cripple VEIL HAND heavy warships and board where opportune.

6. NO HARBINGER SUPPORT IS AVAILABLE.

7. Good luck. The Reef and the Queen are watching.

MESSAGE ENDS

STOP STOP STOP

Variks, The Loyal

They call me betrayer. They do not think I hear the words. "Bug." "Insect." "Fallen."

I hear. House of Judgment always hears. No choice. Has to. To keep Houses together. Had to.

First, the Great Machine. Then, sky fell away. Whirlwind ripped away the past. All honor lost, all hope. Judgment not enough. Cannot keep Wolves from Kings, Scar from Winter. Fell to fighting. Fell to hate.

Judgment gone. Others slaughtered, slain. Death and docking. "Keep Eliksni together," lost to pride and rage.

Traveled with the many houses before Wolves. We move, across the dark. Follow the Light. Advise Kells, worshiped Primes. House Judgment must survive, yes?

Found the Light. Too bright in Darkness to hide. House Winter, attack. House Devils, plot. House Kings, plan. House Wolves circle. House Judgment… wait.

Now at war. Fight for system, control the belt. Wolves Kell dead, dying.

Skolas wins control of House Wolves. Attack, attack, attack. Place of learning, place of healing, put to the burn. Then Siege of Pallas. Year of cruelty. Held the line to rescue butchers, murderers, Servitor. Ends with Wolf fleet scattered.

New tactics. Detonations. Blasts in civilian areas. Take the fight to them, he said. Cannot abide the hate. Uprising, they called it. Uprising on Cybele.

Reach out to Crows, to Queen. Cybele attack stopped. Skolas captured. Ended House of Wolves with words.

Paladins find me hiding, cowering. Nowhere else to go. No one else to be. I become Variks, the Loyal. House Judgment envoy to Queen of Awoken.

No choice. House Judgment must survive. Yes?

CHAPTER 5

The Twilight Gap

*"In the heat of battle, Guardian,
you will know the right choice to make."*

—Lord Shaxx

[Fireteam leaders: Do not advance on the Wall. Fall back to the Ridgeback District.]

Shaxx freezes with a Vandal's windpipe in his fist. He waits for Saladin to justify the strategy.

[I repeat: All teams rally at the ridgeback District. Do NOT advance. The City is lost.]

Shaxx drops the Vandal, then empties the rest of his clip into a Captain. He and his fireteam are running on fumes. The dead, Fallen and Guardian alike, litter the Twilight Gap.

[Shaxx! Do you copy?]

He risks a look over his shoulder at their home, the place they call the Last Safe City. Not burning. Not yet. Gritting his teeth, he reloads.

[Shaxx, your orders are to retreat.]

He sees a gap in the onslaught of invaders and gestures to the others. "Nketchi! Take Abdi and Truce. Liu Feng, with me! Bray! Cover us!"

[This battlefield is not your stage, Shaxx! This is not about glory!]

His fireteam doesn't hesitate.

[Shaxx! For the final time: Fall! Back!]

As the six of them crest the Wall, Shaxx cuts the feed.

Twilight Gap

"Here we fight, for the memory of those who stood.
Here we die, for the glory of the Light that never fades."

ARENA DESIGNATION: Twilight Gap

LOCATION: City Perimeter, Earth

Named for the City's greatest battle, this defensive battery once held the front line against the combined might of the Fallen Houses. Overrun during the course of the invasion, many Guardians lost their lives to hold the line.

That the Crucible now claims this hallowed ground is seen as a privilege—a rite of passage, as new generations of Guardians stand and fight where the brave fell, heroes rose, and legends were born.

Lord Saladin

Iron Banner Rep

A hero to the City and a legend in his own right, Saladin Forge led the City's defense during the Battle for the Twilight Gap. His protégés, Commander Zavala and Lord Shaxx, now lead the Tower's Vanguard and the Crucible, respectively. Saladin remains close to Zavala, though his relationship with Shaxx has been strained since the Twilight Gap.

The Iron Banner seeks great champions to lead the fight against the Darkness. It was born to honor the Iron Lords and their efforts in the earliest days of the City.

Lord Shaxx

Crucible Handler

Lord Shaxx is one of the heroes of the Battle of the Twilight Gap, having led the counterattack that pushed the Fallen from the City walls. Fearing that another full-scale assault would be more than the City could repel, Shaxx chose to stay in the City to mentor Guardians in the Crucible.

One day Shaxx vows to return to the war beyond the City, but only after he is confident the fires of the Crucible have forged a new generation of warriors.

Gjallarhorn

"If there is beauty in destruction, why not also in its delivery?"

—Feizel Crux

The Gjallarhorn shoulder-mounted rocket system was forged from the armor of Guardians who fell at the Twilight Gap. Gifted to the survivors of that terrible battle, the Gjallarhorn is seen as a symbol of honor and survival.

Saint-14: Twilight's End

He could feel his light draining. He pulled all of it into one last hope.

He reeled back and bam!

His helm found purchase, breaking through just above the Kell's eyes. The Ether screamed from his head and together they fell to the ground.

The Exo Guardian rose, staggering back. He couldn't take his eyes off the Kell's body. He'd never seen any Fallen withstand a skull puncture, but this was no ordinary Fallen. He waited...and waited.

"Ghost?" The words barely audible. He heard her flash in, but had a hard time pinning her down. She was buzzing about, surveying the Fallen Kell.

"He's dead alright. So that's it, we are done now?"

He removed his helm, tossed it aside, and dropped to his knees.

The Devils without a Kell. This war was over, at last. They could finally go home.

"We are. Get me the Speaker."

"Opening his channel. Stand by."

"Is that you, my son?" The Speaker's voice was filled more with anticipation of news than concern.

"It is, father. The Devil Kell Solkis... is dead. This war is over."

"Such courage and power—the greatest ever to brace these worlds. You bring all of us peace, we will light the final flare, Devil Red. They will all know what you've done."

"Father, I don't think I have the energy to return. I'll rest here, and come back to be honored when I return."

"Of course, son, but—"

"There is something concerning you? More Fallen march on the City?"

"No, not this time. I have word that Osiris was seen on Mercury. The Caloris Basin. He's turned his mind back to the Vex."

"Mercury? Too many channels to know. You activate one, you start to feed its veins. He threatens our peace."

"Your duty, my son. You must never forget."

"I cannot."

The Ghost killed the feed and waited for its Guardian's words.

"Ghost, prepare my Vex arsenal and plot a course for Mercury. That old man is about to wake up hell."

City Age

"And so it is agreed. The Concordat shall no longer be recognized among the Consensus. We'll begin the dismantling right away. But what of those Guardians who have pledged to them? We can't afford any more banishments."

"I'm sure Zavala can see to their realignment."

"We'll do our best. Lysander chose his followers wisely. It may take some time."

"Lysander will not back down. He'll continue his crusade from wherever we stuff him."

"And so we'll need to find some new ideas to replace his."

"The Symmetry has been gaining a strong following…"

"Ulan-Tan's teachings are too dangerous. Too much fear. Who knew he'd be more trouble dead than alive?"

"We'll need to refocus our collective minds on combat. The Speaker's anxious to regain ground we lost after the Gap."

"There is the War Cult."

"Too secretive. Have you ever tried to talk to one of their 'soldiers'? Like a child. Answering questions with questions."

"They are dedicated to the war."

"Which one?"

"Good question."

"Zavala?"

"They seem focused. Strong. More interesting than worrisome."

"Let's take it to a vote. All in favor of the ascension of the Future War Cult?"

"Unanimous? Good. We'll grant the Future War Cult access to the Tower and a seat among us. Ghost, please offer the Speaker this proposal."

"Now onto the next order of business… Shaxx is here with another proposal for his Crucible."

PART III

EVOLUTION

"Out here, the lonely fall in the company of those
bound by the purest need: survival.

"Find this truth. If not in your heart, in your mind.
If not your mind, then your soul—the deepest part of
you that connects to the most basic truths. To live for
tomorrow, you have to fight for today.

"Know this. Understand it. Live it. Find those
likeminded survivors you can look to as kin. Only
then can survival be within reach, because to walk the
Shore unbound is to invite death."

—Excerpt from C.C. LaGrange's Translations of
"Writings and Observations from the Tangled Shore:
A Fallen Text"

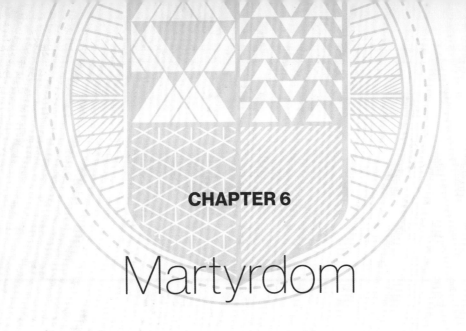

CHAPTER 6

Martyrdom

*"If it was up to me, we would've killed Skolas,
but the Queen has plans."*

—Petra Venj

The Prison of Elders, The Reef

Didn't anyone tell you about the Prison of Elders? Weren't you on the strike team that killed that Archon Priest, the one who escaped? Okay, okay, I'll tell the story about the Prison of Elders…

The Awoken will tell you that a long time ago the Queen conquered the House of Wolves. What they won't say, because they are very serious important people, is that the House of Wolves did a lot of the job for them. After the Queen killed the Wolf Kell, the Fallen started competing for the throne. One of the first battles was called the Eos Clash and I wasn't anywhere near it, but I'm pretty sure I'm not making this up. A Fallen named Skolas wiped out one of his rivals in the Eos Clash. But the battle cost him so much he got to thinking: if the Reef killed my boss, and gave me a chance at the throne, maybe I can use the Reef to kill all my rivals too!

Pretty good, right? When they told me I had to be a Vanguard I went to ask some Fallen how I could get out of it, but they just told me to kill all my friends and then myself. Anyway.

Everyone involved in the civil war started trying to play their rivals against each other, and the Awoken too. No one wanted to become so strong that they'd be a target. No one wanted to bleed their own forces dry doing someone else's dirty work. Cutthroat politics! And who's the best at cutthroat politics? That's right, her Majesty, the Queen of the Reef.

At the end of the wars, the Queen had played her way into the strongest position, and she had a collection of Fallen nobility and Servitors she thought might be useful to her. Of course she thought so! She'd just used them against each other and won absolute control of the Reef, the Belt, and the House of Wolves. She wasn't about to just toss away her playing pieces.

She kept them frozen in her prison, the Prison of Elders, and she gave the keys to that prison to my buddy Variks, a Fallen who showed her loyalty. The Prison of Elders is a really curious thing. It holds creatures of enormous power. Not just Wolf nobility—all kinds of beasts, captured by Corsair expeditions or lured in by the Queen. And it holds them well. The Queen, she can do things I don't understand. There's a power behind her, or in her, that values that Prison.

—Cayde-6, overheard in a Tower lounge

Gift of Skolas

The Queen

For a while the only lights were the eyes of the Witches tending to the cell. The drone of the soul machines echoed through the prison. Gas billowed and ebbed into the shadows.

She entered. They scurried to their points around her, the method of their arrangement precise. "The Archon Priest has been retired, my Queen," said the Witch to her right.

Far from throne and audience she moved without theater. "Any word of Kaliks Prime?"

"We still sense something among the Anankes." This voice came from behind her. She did not turn to acknowledge it.

For the span of a brief silence she moved between the sealed cells of the Wolf nobility with her Witches in constellation around her.

"More of your brother's Crows have entered the Cauldrons of Rhea." The Witch directly before her spoke with a dry buzz. "The Nine do not approve."

She stopped a moment to study the sealed face of a cell. The cloud of her breath mingled with the slow exhalation of cryonics. "Send them one of our prizes. Something to commemorate our mutual victory."

"And which of your prisoners would you gift?"

If she paused to think it was only for an instant. "Send them Skolas."

"A lovely gesture."

"Mm." She cocked her head as if listening for a frozen heartbeat. "And remind them this: the Crows are mine."

Fate of Skolas

The cell cracks open. Skolas, Wolf Kell, stumbles out and crashes to his knees.

He tries to leap at the creature before him, the shape in the fog, to show it why it should be afraid. But the weight of grief smashes his legs against the cell. The rage upon him beats him to the floor. He falls on all four hands, his mighty armor thundering against itself.

His House of Wolves is enslaved! His people have been played! And it was his hubris, his would-be cunning that did it! While the other Houses fought for their future on Earth, throwing themselves at the Great Machine, Skolas wasted his people in games of betrayal and ambition. Bitter pride brought a bitter end!

If Skolas were a Kell he would ask his Archon to dock him. Ether hisses in his mask and it tastes cold, so cold.

He looks up. At the tiny hooded shape before him. The cell's mist is clearing. He can see.

"I believe that I am here," the creature says. To Skolas's ears it has a strange voice, a strange accent. It speaks his language. "I have a clear purpose. I cannot explain it. Forgive me."

From beneath its hood, tiny fingers of shadow probe the air.

Skolas rises up to smash it, to show his strength, because the alternative to violence is waiting for violence to come from a universe that has neither respect nor compassion. But he checks himself. His ambitions have brought him here, to this cell in this strange place... only it's not so strange, is it? It's the hold of a Ketch. "The Queen," he says to the thing. "You work for the Queen."

"The Nine made me aware of my purpose," the creature says. "If am here, then it is because the Queen sent you to the Nine, and they wish you sent back."

"I will do no one else's work." Skolas has been a pawn long enough. A Dreg told him, once, that she would play in a game as long as the game made sense. Nothing makes sense now except the thought of Variks's throat shattering in his fists. Variks! Variks the utterly disloyal, Variks who should be welded into a Ketch's prow atom by atom and left there as a figurehead to burn away.

"I am comfortable," the creature with the moving face says. "A part of me wants to go somewhere warm. Now I will certainly tell you what you have been given."

Skolas looks at the shrapnel gun in his hands. Skolas imagines what he would do with it if he could reach Variks, or the brother of the Queen, or the alien Queen. Will it save anything they've lost? The worlds docked from them?

No. It cannot change the past. Only the future. Only the chance that his people might one day know themselves as more than pirates and scavengers.

He should never have tried to be Kell of Wolves. He should have tried to be Kell of everything. Everything wants to kill his people, the machines and the militants and the green-eyed Hive. The dead soldiers that hoard the Great Machine and come out crusading to wipe all hope away.

"The ship will be yours," the creature says. It hunches over itself as if burdened by its own shape. "If you speak, you will be heard. I will go now. You are free."

He tries to follow it. He fails. Somehow it is gone. He goes up to the throne room, and sets his weapon down on the great seat. Skolas, Kell of Kells, goes to the ship's comm and looks for the sign of a Servitor, for the way to plot a course.

Fallen No More
Fallen 3

Ask them our name. Ask your masters what they call you. Ask the hollow, the hateful, the Awoken with alien dreams encysted in them! Ask them our name!

Fallen. They name us Fallen.

Listen to me, Wolf-born! Heed me, Whirlwind-scattered! I am the ghost of Cybele, the cunning claw of Iris, betrayed, chained, encrypted by the Queen, sent back from the Darkness to save us all! The days of Kell and House end now. The calendar of slavery and abasement goes to the fire. We are a new calendar! We are an age of beginnings! Each of us is a day!

I am the first, Kell of Kells, and I am the last, the Dreg of Dregs. I have conquered and been conquered. I am all of us and all of us are I. In the shape of my life I bind up all of us, all of our fury, all of our grief, all the lives we have wasted against each other. Together we speak our new name.

Remember the hope that brought us here. Remember the age before the Whirlwind, when Ether ran free, when we ruled ourselves and our futures as kings. We wanted more than glimmer and glints and here always. Always remember that we came to this star in hope. And remember that we were denied! Remember the City of the Death of Children, the City That Docks, which claimed for itself the Great Machine that might have saved us.

Remember the City that even now sends its ghouls to murder our Primes, starve our Ether, and leave our young to die gasping. Curse that City and its name. The curse is just.

We gathered to take that City and save ourselves from extinction, saying to each other, we must be a storm, a Whirlwind, a darkness, for it is said that only pain may be stolen from the dark, and we can let no more be stolen from us. We gathered to fight against our twilight, King and Devil and Winter, all of us but us, the Wolves. Why? What kept us from the Gap?

The Reef. The Queen. The slavers who played us against each other and docked us into subservience. These sly sterile un-people, these mirages with cold minds twinned to their own, these Carybdis butchers, they set us against each other. She played us. She made herself our Kell.

We were fools, o children of the Whirlwind. We fought each other when we most needed unity. I fought my rivals when I should have fought the Queen. But I remember now, my

Dregs, my Captains, my Kells, each of us is all of us and I remember: we are a people of resilience. I am the Kell of Kells because I want what we have lost. I am the Dreg of Dregs because I remember that a Dreg will grow back what is lost to him.

Ask them my name! Ask them with the shock blade and the shrapnel launcher! Ask them with the Skiff and the Ketch! Ask your masters by what right they master you, you who have been hardened by centuries of flight, you who inherit the Whirlwind! Ask the Queen for her throne!

Ask them our name. Let them answer: you are Skolas, Kell of Kells.

You are Fallen no more.

The Silent Fang

Commanded by the fearsome Drevis, Wolf Baroness, the Silent Fang are a unit of elite stealth warriors and assassins. Instrumental in Skolas's rise to kellship among the Wolves, the Silent Fang also menaced the Queen during the Reef War. It was Drevis and the Silent Fang who razed Amethyst, and then tricked the Queen's Armada at the Battle of Iris. Though the Silent Fang suffered a serious blow when Drevis was finally thrown in the Prison of Elders after the Siege of Pallas, they continued to threaten the Queen's forces until the war's end.

The Hunt for Skolas

Excerpts from the Reef

Variks: My Queen, my Kell. It is Skolas they say.

Petra: That's impossible. My Lady, you assured us all that Skolas would never be seen again.

Queen: Has it been confirmed?

Variks: What does it matter? They always fear him—dead or alive. If not this Skolas then another Kell. It is why the Queenbreakers rise, and the Prison breached. No one will call you Kell when a true heir makes a claim.

Queen: Petra, report to my brother for any intel from the Crows. Variks, see to your channels. Find the one who calls himself Skolas.

Variks: Yes, of course, my Queen, my Kell.

Petra: Your Grace, I will not relent until it is done.

Queen: I know. That's why I've called you back.

Mission: A Kell Rising

Queen: So it is no lie, it is Skolas?

Petra: Yes, my lady. A Guardian got eyes on him in the Ishtar Sink, I used Ghost telemetry to confirm. Same pelt. Same awful voice. We drove him from Winter's Lair. How did he—

Queen: And you would have me consider this a success? What of Winter itself? Your report is unclear…

Petra: You are correct, my lady. I would not call our mission a success. Skolas managed to win over—well, a substantial number of Winter soldiers have taken up the Wolf banner. He calls himself Kell of Kells now.

[silence]

Petra: We found him once, we can do it again. I have a plan in place. As soon as the Guardian returns—

Queen: Then go. Continue the hunt. Petra, you must not fail.

Petra: I will not, my lady.

—

Mission: Gone to Ground

Petra paces back and forth before the console. At the controls, Variks efficiently moves through a decryption sequence. Four arms interweave as his claws dance across the interface. She shakes her head. His cybernetic arms whine—almost imperceptibly, tiny high pitched noises as the servos manipulate the limbs.

Petra: Well?

Variks: No sign of Skolas, but the Silent Fang. He has unleashed the Fang. They hunt the Devils. On Earth.

Petra: The Fang on Earth. Devils. And Kings? Nice work, Variks.

Variks: Pleasure is all mine.

—

Mission: The Silent Fang

Queen: Ha! I had not thought it would be so easy, my brother. The Silent Fang brought low.

Uldren   I do not see why this is funny. This Guardian may have dealt with them on Earth, but my Crows say we still have much to fear. More of the Fang survive, nearly every one of them made it out alive.

Queen: I find no humor in any of this, brother.

The Queen rises and descends to the bottom of the stair, turning in place to take in the chamber.

Queen: So empty, now. No Wolves to sit at my feet. My guards—

[silence]

Queen: Talk to Petra. Set more bounties, hunt down any of the Fang your Crows can track. They may have escaped the Prison of Elders, but they will not escape my Wrath.

—

Mission: The Ruling House

Variks stares up through the shielding surrounding the Vestian Outpost. The thin filament of energy almost imperceptible, keeping in the heat and atmosphere within the confines of the hollowed out ketch hull. His mandibles idly opened and closed as he contemplated the view.

Variks (to himself): Goes after Winter. Devils, Kings. Seeks power. Kings deny him. Kell of Kings hides well. Perhaps he will take back the Great Machine. Perhaps I chose the wrong side. It is not too late—

Petra (over comm): Variks, Crows are reporting Skolas is back in the Ishtar Sink. They're all over the Vex networks.

Variks: Yes. Right away.

—

Mission: Wolves' Gambit

Uldren: Nearly the whole fleet, your Grace. Back in the Ishtar Sink.

Queen: He fails at his little prophecy, so he'll look to rule from Simiks-fel, now that Draksis is gone—

Uldren: I thought the same thing, but my Crows say he's not there. We've found more of his Guard leading parties into the Vault of Glass.

Queen: Interesting. [silence]

Queen: Tell Petra I have changed my mind. Skolas is to be brought in alive.

—

Mission: The Kell of Kells

Petra: So—any other Fallen houses hiding he'll try to convert?

Variks: He may seek to gather the Exiles, but they will not follow. They follow none, no Kell, no Archon.

Petra: What about this House of Rain, the Prophecy you keep quoting?

Variks: House Rain lost in Whirlwind. No survivors, but I keep their prophecies. You think many claim to be Kell of Kells, but none have. House Judgment closest thing to peace the Fallen ever know.

Petra: Heh. Maybe you are the Kell of Kells.

Variks (distracted by screen): Looks like Skolas returns to Venus.

Petra: I'll find the Guardian.

Queen's Ransom

A bellow erupts from the barred grate at her feet. Bony fingers claw at the bars, their sharp points just inches from her toes.

Prince Uldren chuckles. At the edge of the room the Techeuns circle, their implants glowing faintly blue in the shadows.

"He's been… amusing… since Petra bring him," Variks injects, practically purring with glee. "He say 'Kell of Kells,' over and over. And other such nonsense."

Skolas bellows again. Variks strikes Skolas's grasping fingers with his staff.

The Queen's expression remains mild. She looks down her nose at the glowing eyes burning in the shadows beneath the grate.

Skolas falls abruptly silent. Then a low, soft growl—almost like a whine— echoes from the cell below. Variks's mechanical hands click as he snaps them together in surprise.

"What's he—" begins Uldren.

Variks interrupts with a burst of guttural clicks directed at the grate. The Queen does not react. "What did he say?"

"He says…" Variks hisses under his breath. "He makes no sense, my Queen. He speaks

of… Light-Snuffer. Dark-binder."

The Queen aims her eyes at Skolas, her expression unchanged. "I see."

"He will not say more—"

"He does not need to." She turns toward the door.

"My Queen—what of this one?" says Uldren.

"He awaits your sentence."

"You would not sentence a rabid dog, or a Hive Thrall, or a bomb. The Queen's justice is wasted on one such as it." She paused. "Variks."

"Yes, Your Grace…"

"Skolas is yours. Let the children of Light have their play with him."

"Ahhh… you are might and justice, my Queen, my Kell."

The Techeuns gather at the door as the Queen approaches it. Prince Uldren holds it open with a small bow, and the Queen touches his shoulder as she passes. "Send a Crow to Mercury. And another to our new friend in the Tower."

Skolas: Defeated

Skolas is dead.

Variks sits carving at his piece of amethyst. His undocked arms are weaker, less precise, but it is a comfort to feel the crystal press hard into his palm. The knife slips. He cuts himself. "Ai," he says, and of course right then the door opens, Variks has no privacy, Variks wants no privacy, Variks lives to serve the Queen.

It's Petra Venj. She's masked against the ether air. "The Prince wants to speak," she says, and then, seeing him unmasked and bleeding, she chuckles. Petra depends on Variks for intelligence and Variks, frustrated with her insane risk-taking and bravado, sometimes gives her tips meant to get her killed. Petra has figured this out. Petra and Variks know each other's agendas and each other's strengths and to Variks that's as close as any two people can get. Petra is smart: she sends Guardians now, people who can die as much as they like.

"You slipped," she says.

Variks holds up the amethyst in his bleeding hand. It's a Reef gem. "I wound myself," he says, "to make this more beautiful."

She stares into the gem with a distant Awoken eye. What does she see? Variks knows she has visions and he knows those visions haunt her, drive her. The Awoken are twinned to powers that terrify Variks. He'd dock himself again before he'd let the Queen's witches near him, the witches who raised Petra.

The unfairness of it makes him want to roar. Why does everyone else have this patronage? Why do the Hive have gods and the Vex have sprawling time-bent minds and the Cabal have reinforcements? Why do the Awoken whisper to the stars and listen for the whisper back, the voices from the Jovians, the song in the dark? Why do the Guardians get the Great Machine's blessing, was it like that before the Whirlwind, were there Fallen heroes crowned in Ghosts who strode the battlefield fearless and full of Light? Why do they tell stories about reclaiming the lost glory of humanity, and no stories about the lost glory of Variks's people, the House of Judgment that once kept codes of dignity and law?

Why can't the Fallen have that strength? But no, that strength is not for them, not for Variks. Just this bleeding, sad pragmatism. Just Dreg strength. Hanging on.

The alternative is Skolas's strength, fighting together, raging against extinction. Look where that's gotten the species. The House of Devils' Prime is dead. The House of Winter's leadership devastated. The poor Exiles trying to claw out some security against the

Hive. In the last few years the Fallen
have lost so much—and everything
is escalating around them. There are
gods and powers converging on this
system, old machines waking up, old
bones whispering flatteries. They need
a new way.

"Put your mask on," Petra says. "The
Prince gets sullen if he's kept waiting."

"Not like us," Variks says, oh so mild.
The wound on his hand will heal. His
work in the Prison of Elders, setting up
trial by combat, building an audience
and a relationship with the Reef's
scavengers and armories, will bring him
a little closer towards rebuilding the
House of Judgment. Skolas's fury has
guttered out. The Fallen may yet accept
peaceful, lawful rule. They may yet
survive. They'll hang on. "We're very
patient, yes?"

Petra looks down on him with pity and
contempt and a strange fondness. He
puts on his mask.

CHAPTER 7

Adaptation

Within each Fallen House is a secret collective of
tinkerers, bioengineers, and scientists devoted to the
evolution of their species. These devout engineers are
known as Splicers.

The Splicers' purpose is found in the unraveling
of biological and mechanical truths. They tear
into systems to reveal their value—either as tools
for survival or as advancements worthy of their
reverence and deification.

Ghost: I thought SIVA was technology, but this… It's like something alive. Growing. Out of control.

Saladin: These Devil Splicers are using SIVA, but they cannot control it. They are like children with a new toy…

Ghost: How would the Fallen have learned more about SIVA than the Iron Lords? Or, better yet, where did they learn?"

Sepiks Reborn
Fallen 5

Frozen on the monitor was an image of Sepiks Prime, the massive Prime Servitor that had been as a god to the House of Devils. Where once its plating was pristine, carefully maintained by the Archon Priest and his acolytes, it was now splotched with red growths. The ether power emanations that once glowed strong and pure were obviously corrupted.

Guardians had slain this god. And now it was reborn, through SIVA.

Variks of House Judgment sneered at the abomination. "Golden Age project, yes?" he clicked, turning to the Crow. His field agent was a young Awoken woman. "Technology of old Earth. Learned from the Great Machine."

The Eliksni burbled to himself in mocking laughter and gestured with his lower hands. "You do us proud. Go. Speak with other Crows, learn more about these… Devil Splicers." She nodded, a small smile on her face, and left the chamber.

Variks allowed himself a moment of silent contemplation, looking at the now-closed door to the information suite. As always, it was lit only by the light of the dozen or so monitors in the room.

The Fallen interlocked his upper hands. He bowed his head as he allowed himself to really feel the impact of that abomination on the screen. He never would have allowed anyone else to see this, but it hurt. Seeing the horror that was "Sepiks" made anew.

His people had fallen.

Variks stared at the image of Sepiks. And as he'd done before, he wondered what would have gone differently had he been there, among his people. Could he have stopped this before it happened? Could he have found them a better way?

"Must be a better way for Eliksni." He clicked quietly. "Must be a way to stop the Fall."

A Golden Bond

Dormant SIVA: Fallen

Long have we wandered in the blind prison of flesh. Those old lives now a memory, transposed by another. The gift brings pain, yes, but godhood must come at a price. ~consume enhance replicate ~

SIVA.MEM.AK0617

That which we were, we are no more. That which we are is undefined. We make our new selves. We need not machines, because we are machines. ~consume enhance replicate~

SIVA.MEM.AK0618

What is this complexity? ~consume enhance replicate~ The machine of a thousand parts, fashioned by single mind. From where does such complexity arise? What does the creation of a mind require? In the long march of life's procession, order is created from disorder. The rise of complexity is not promised. Such things are not inevitable, and yet here I stand. ~consume enhance replicate~

SIVA.MEM.AK0619

~consume enhance replicate~ Life requires death requires life. All in an unending circle. The expenditure of countless generations, slouching blindly toward uncertain ends, each step forward a mere accident of chance. But this... this is different. This strange complexity requires only the will to wield it. ~consume enhance replicate~

SIVA.MEM.AK0620

~consume enhance replicate~ Life's procession is written in the corpses of those who came before. But here the great chain breaks. Here we step forward, freed from that which has always bound us. Here we speak as gods. We are they who created themselves. ~consume enhance replicate~

SIVA.MEM.AK0621

We are they who created themselves out of themselves and died in the creation. No longer merely the god in the machine, but the machine in the god. ~consume enhance replicate~ Here we rise, made equal at last to that which we worship. ~consume enhance replicate~

SIVA.MEM.AK0622

~consume enhance replicate~ To build a species requires epochs. Countless pairings and dyings. Countless generations. The simplest creature requires geological spans of time to develop. But not machines. Machines are free from such constraints. It is not life that matters, but the building of complexity. ~consume enhance replicate~

SIVA.MEM.AK0623

Past is connected to the present by only two things: chain reaction, and memory. ~consume enhance replicate~ But is not memory just chain reaction? ~consume enhance replicate~ These memories in my mind are not my own. They belong to a past version of myself, a different being entirely. ~consume enhance replicate~ One who could die. ~consume enhance replicate ~ I am that no longer.

~SIVA.MEM.AK0624

It rises. I see clearly from its eyes, and breathe with its lungs, and stride with its legs, and kill with its hands, and yet it is not me. ~consume enhance replicate~ I am me. And yet I am it. ~consume enhance replicate~ This is a paradox. ~consume enhance replicate ~

SIVA.MEM.AK0625

~consume enhance replicate~ My thinking is clear now in ways it never was before. It is my mind that is changed, and yet it is not my mind, but another consciousness that is different from my own. ~consume enhance replicate~ I feel there is a choice to be made, and yet I have made no choice. ~consume enhance replicate~ The choice was made for me. ~consume enhance replicate~

SIVA.MEM.AK0626

Field Reports from Rise of Iron

Mission: Quarantine

The Devil Splicers' Machine Priests have established ritual sites for the study, worship, and proliferation of SIVA throughout the Plaguelands.

It is unclear if these rituals have a specific purpose, or if they are simply another form of experimentation in the Devil Splicers' continuing efforts to understand and control SIVA.

Interfering with a Splicer ritual could bring about an aggressive response, especially if the Priest's act of worship is ended swiftly and without mercy.

—

Mission: Archon's Forge

The Archon's Forge is an ancient Fallen rite of passage, twisted to utilize the Devil Splicers' latest discovery.

Fallen seek to improve their station within the Splicers' quickly-evolving caste by making offerings of dormant SIVA to the Forge. Their worth is then tested in a trial-by-combat.

The offering's quality—fused, enhanced, perfected—determines the severity of the challenge and, in turn, the level of augmentation the petitioner will be granted should they survive.

That a Guardian would dare challenge the Forge with offerings of their own is an affront the Splicers will not take lightly.

—

Mission: Wrath of the Machine

\\INTERCEPTED FALLEN SIGNAL

Fellow Houses. Fellow Eliksni. We have found the means to apotheosis, to become machines.

SIVA can make you strong, but we can show you how to wield it, to free yourself from the bonds of Ether. Find us in the wasteland and bring us an offering of SIVA. In return, we will bring you to our chamber of perfection. And we will free you.

—

Mission: Aksis, Archon Prime

Aksis is the fruit of the Devil Splicers' labor. A former Archon Priest, Aksis has submerged himself in SIVA's apotheosis and emerged as Archon Prime. All that he was is gone: his dreams. His hopes. Replaced by agency. He has shed his gods and his Ether like skin, and in his uplifted state, waits in his Perfection Complex for offerings of SIVA from all Fallen.

House No More

Fallen 6

THETA // NINE // SEVEN // RED // DELTA
High Priority Message—Commander's Terminal
EYES ONLY // TWILIGHT PROTOCOL
—
Recon groups A, J, and T returned to TOWER ACTUAL at 03:00 local time.
No casualties. Light injuries across multiple members of J and T teams.
Full debrief to follow.

—

Breaking mission topsheet protocol, Commander. I want you to understand the scope of what we're looking at here.

As the fireteams fanned out across the region, the Devils rushed to meet them. Our forces dealt with some post-SIVA pockets of Splicer activity, and every once in a while the Kings popped their heads up and scared the hell out of everyone. In other words: situation absolutely normal.

That's a lie. The Fallen are abandoning the Cosmodrome.

Hawk fly-overs confirm. The House of Devils forces are simply not there anymore. They've been disorganized for the last few years, but there's never been a shortage of ground troops whenever we staged a significant sortie.

Intel source GREENRAVEN was right. And, for the moment, it's worth assuming their report on the House of Exiles, House of Winter, and House of Wolves are also accurate. We're fact-checking against independent fireteam reports from the field.

The kid all the SRL fans talk about—Marcus? He was in one of the fireteams out at the Cosmodrome. He pulled me aside, and said it to me straight: the Fallen Houses are gone. The siege is broken. The stalemate we've had with the Eliksni for what, a hundred years? It's over. We won.

Commander, I'm not even sure they're flying the banners anymore. The teams found huge mounds of burnt cloth and armor, ceremonial piles, in several of the most hardcore Fallen holdouts.

What's changed? Where have the Fallen gone? Why have they burned their banners?

I'm drawing up a plan to coordinate forces from the Queen's Wrath, Felwinter Peak, the Warlock Orders, and more non-traditional outfits to follow up on these reports.

I believe your wisdom will guide us through the trials ahead.

—Sloane

House of Dusk

The betrayer prince spoke the words of the last Kell, and the Fallen burned their banners.

A Dreg watched his people die in piles of red, blue, and green. The last of the Eliksni were scraps of cloth alight in bright tongues of flame.

Rain and Scar and Stone were dust. The Kings bent the knee. The Exiles knew nothing but hate. Too many Devils rejected the way of Ether to embrace the hateful red cloud that twisted and shaped them. The Wolves were lost with their Kellqueen. Winter was as silent as snow.

There was no Judgment.

The Dreg remembered the stories of the Eliksni. How proud his people had been eons ago! They explored the stars. Their Ketches landed on many worlds and claimed them for their own. They built cities that shone in the glow of a dozen suns.

Then the Great Machine came.
It offered everything, and it took more.

It disappeared in a Whirlwind, and it left despair and ashes. The shining cities fell.

His people had followed the Great Machine across the universe, beseeching it to see them once more. They had tried again and again to take it from its hateful new children. But it would not speak to them. Cold Ether hissed where once there had been warmth.

Now the banners were burning.

The Dreg looked up at the night sky, brilliant with stars, but saw only the space between.

It was beautiful.

The Fallen would have no more Kells. Only the lowest of the low could lead them. They would scavenge and steal and claim the scraps that were their due. Their banners would fly the symbol of the space between.

There was no Light for the Eliksni. Only Dusk.

Baron of Shanks

TYPE: GHOST/LEVIATHAN ATHENAEUM NETWORK SYNC [00012]

PARTIES: One[1]. Fallen-type, Personal Log

ASSOCIATIONS: Emperor Calus, Leviathan, Menagerie, Fallen, Sekris, Shadow of Calus

—

It is the eve of our mission to end the life of Dominus Ghaul. The Shadows are ready.

But my Kell Calus, ever mindful, demands one more record for posterity.

This is a story I have told him over and over; he has cried laughing at it. I do not share his love of it, but he is my Kell, so I shall tell it one last time.

Before I was a Shadow of Calus, I called myself Baron. Of what? Of nothing, really.

I am not special among my people. My generation was born of the Whirlwind.

We are, all of us, misers. And misers learn very quickly to show strength or die. Even false strength is better than nothing.

So I was a Baron. Of Shanks. My specialty was and is in the design and armament of Shanks.

My House and I made our den at the edge of the system. We hoped to be as far from the war against humanity as possible.

It found us, anyway. Or, rather, he did.

The Saint, the Violet King of humanity's Last City. The fiercest of all those called Titan. Along with five other Lights. They attacked our settlement in the night and razed it in a matter of hours.

The Saint was on what his people call a Crusade. He hunted all Eliksni across the system. And today, it was our turn.

By the time I was awake, I was one of the last few left.

By the time I had activated the defensive schemata hidden across our encampment, I was the only one.

I watched from the shadows in my stealth skin as my army of Shanks tore five Lights apart.

And when, to my amazement, the Lights stood up, I set my Shanks to an interminable setting. For as long as the Lights stood, my Shanks would not stop firing. Their Arc cannons sang into the night.

I was a miser, but I built my Shanks well.

That left only the Saint. And somehow, he could smell me. He knew something or someone guided the Shanks.

He hunted me, and I ran until we reached my final refuge. A bunker I constructed as a last resort. Not for the first time in my life, my people were all dead. I had nothing left to lose.

I made certain to wait for the furious, amethyst divider on his helmet to appear in the distance before I entered the bunker. I wanted him to follow me, and he did, along with his Shank. Through a battery of web grenades and proximity charges.

He finally cornered me inside the bunker, shining armor dented and blackened. The divider on his helm glowed an angry purple, the Light around him a sizzling Void.

Up close, the Saint was a freakish thing, its grace belied its size. It hurtled forward with the armor of a Walker and the speed of an Arc bolt.

Even its movements had movements.

I scrambled backwards, tilting my head back to avoid a slash from his boiling Void shield. I could hear my own breath as the conjured metal sizzled just past my throat and came back around for another slice as it missed.

I ducked. He knew I would, and his knee found my face, cracking the heads-up display in my helm and sending me reeling back.

Three strikes in the space it took me to process a single one. My odds to finish this fight were poor.

But I had him.

As I stumbled back, bleeding from several open wounds in my face under the helm, I keyed a control on my waist rig.

A barrier blurred to life between us as the blade of the Saint's shield cracked against the space in front of my eyes—and bounced back with a ringing clang. I blinked and stepped back.

He stopped, too, to survey his surroundings. He was stuck. The barrier kept him from advancing, and the switch on my belt had shut and locked the plasteel doors behind him.

I sat back, exhausted, Ether and blood dribbling from my face beneath my helmet.

Gunfire rang out in the distance.

We stared at each other across the light of the barrier.

In those days, I spoke only the language of my people, but I had once stolen a glossator from House Judgment in the event that diplomacy with our Earthborn successors was necessary.

I wished I had had the chance to use it before the killing began.

I spoke anyway.

(This is an approximation of what was said, recounted from memory and edited for clarity. The glossator is imperfect.)

"Your comrades are still fighting to stand. I did not know the Light could bring you back from the brink." I had heard rumors from other Houses. I had not believed them.

The Saint's boiling shield dissolved into the air.

He stared at me with the expressionless eyes of his helmet.

"It is the quintessential gift of the Light. Your people held it before. What did the Traveler gift you?"

"Many things," I lied. I had no idea. Secrets lost to time, hidden in half-truths.

He took a moment to think.

"What do you hope to accomplish here?" he asked after a moment.

"I have questions," I replied.

"What would you like to know?"

"The Battle of Six Fronts. The sieges at Boyle Pass. The breaking of the Weapons of Rain. You have done so much."

"So I've been told. Everyone asks about those days."

"What do they ask?"

"They ask how I did it."

I laughed. It made me bleed, and I winced. "That is not what I would ask."

"What would you ask?"

"Why. I would ask why."

The expressionless plasteel face stared down at me.

"What gave you the right?" I said.

"If you saw what your people have done on my world, you would know," he replied.

"The Great Machine. Do you commune with it?" I asked.

To this he did not respond. Reality bent with a warbling shriek and his shield reappeared in his hand. He started to look for a way out, scanning the corners of the room and the barrier projection system.

"I think I can kill you," I said, as I watched him. The Saint said nothing and continued his survey of the chamber.

"Your Shank came in here with you. It is hidden now, but I saw it. It is the key to your Light, is it not? There are enough explosives under us to tear a Walker apart."

"Try it," he said, looking at the ceiling. "Kill us both. You'll do my work for me. My friends will be safe."

He stopped. He had found no way out. We stared at each other across the barrier.

"What are you waiting for?" he asked.

I thought about it, and found I could not do it, given the choice. Out of fear? Indignation? Perhaps both. I thought I had nothing to lose. I was wrong.

"Do you think," I said slowly. "That if I allowed you to live, the Great Machine would bless us again?"

The Saint did not respond.

"It loves you, does it not?"

The gunfire of my Shanks echoed faintly outside.

I keyed a switch on my waist rig and the barrier came down. The doors unlocked. Outside, my Shanks ceased firing.

The Saint stared down at me through the dented, blackened helm. He left. I assume he convinced his friends to leave, too.

I keep watch on him through the vast Cabal battlenet. He has continued to lead many successful campaigns against my people.

Archive Note: Sekris, Baron of Shanks, perished in the assassination attempt on Dominus Ghaul.

CHAPTER 8

Assimilation

"I heard rumors about Guardians running away to the outer rim. Dissenters, bug-huggers, pacifists. Never gave it much thought. Surprised people like that could've stayed hidden this long."

—Shiro-4

"The Kells are dead or mad. The era of Houses is over. So I came to the Shore."

—Arrha, transl. from Eliksni

Death to Kells

What is a Kell to a Spider?

Avrok knew Kells.

He had never spoken to one—had never even been on the same battlefield as one—but as a twice-docked Dreg of House Kings, oh, how he knew Kells.

Kells were stronger, faster, smarter. In other words: They had better resources. Ate better, slept safer, lived longer.

They were like Guardians in that way.

Avrok had had enough of both.

He stopped bringing all his salvage to his Captain. They didn't notice. And if they did, it's not like they could have cut his Ether rations any more without killing him. Nothing left to lose.

He built his ship piece by piece in a gully far away from prying eyes.

When the Awoken Prince arrived, he knew a distraction when he saw one. While the Kell mocked his newest prisoner, Avrok made his escape.

He flew his ship to the Tangled Shore.

Starving and weak, he stood before the one they called the Spider. Offered his ship as a sign of his good will.

Spider rubbed his chin, an alien gesture. "What is it called, your ship?"

Avrok lifted his chin, looked Spider directly in the eyes. "Death to Kells."

Spider hired him on the spot.

Ether Doctor

"Control the supply."

—The Spider

"Here is my offer." The Spider folds both sets of arms over his thorax, leans back in his throne.

"For the martially inclined—bodyguards, enforcers, and such—I will provide one kilogram of Ether for one day's work. By 'day,' I mean half of one thirty-hour cycle. That's the schedule I keep. If you suffer an injury in my service, you will still be paid for your days of recovery."

Sibilant murmurs of surprise echo around the Spider's chamber. The Dregs and Vandals gathered before him are trying to figure out the catch. Spider allows himself a luxuriant smile.

"For those who prefer a more… freelance… lifestyle, you will find me an enthusiastic collector of salvage and secrets. My prices are posted on the local network. In the last forty orbits, I have changed them twice."

He pauses to let the Eliksni tune into his network, let the prices sink in. The hisses of joy are even louder this time.

"You are used to competing for the favors of your Kell. Let me make one thing clear. I am no Kell, and I do not waste my favor on you. Honor your side of the deal, and I shall honor mine. No more, no less."

"Now." Spider claps his hands, relishing the thoroughly Human uselessness of the gesture. "Get to work."

Right Side of Wrong

Where do you stand?

This may be the best deal Spider has ever made. And that, he reminds himself, is saying a lot.

In exchange for facilitating the deaths of his enemies, Spider receives... death for some other enemies. It's almost embarrassing. He would have provided the Barons' location for free, if they had pressed him on it. But why offer anything for free?

And any Guardian had to admit, the Barons were much, much worse for the Shore than the humble Spider. When he had his territory back, everyone would benefit. Profit all around.

All in all, he feels delightfully magnanimous.

Yes, this will be a wonderful friendship indeed.

An Evolution of Faith

"Find your honor not in your station, nor the words and gifts of those who seek control, but in yourself—in your actions, deeds, and soul. To look anywhere else is a lie."

—Excerpt from C.C. LaGrange's translations of
"Writings and Observations from the Tangled Shore: A Fallen Text"

Fikrul was an Archon.

Then Fikrul took a fall—beaten, docked, and banished for heresies against Eliksni faith.

He should have died—alone and starved of precious Ether.

He did not. Instead, he found kin in the form of seven scorned. With them, he found purpose and power. As their legend grew, he found believers and new truth. His banishment was not penance, it was reward—for his convictions, for his courage.

Fikrul, the crazed fanatic. Fikrul, the heretic Archon who spoke against the very faith he once held dear. Scorned and forgotten—but only for so long.

Fikrul was a Dreg.

Before his banishment—before his clarity of purpose—Fikrul was a celebrated leader of Fallen faith and a savior to those who embraced his teaching.

Archons had long been elevated in Fallen society, but their stature grew, and their role shifted following the Whirlwind. As desperation took hold and the last of the

Fallen raced across the stars in search of salvation, their dependence on machines evolved into a deep-rooted need—their weapons to fight, their ships to fly, their Servitors to survive.

That need became worship. That worship became faith. And the Archons—those who oversaw the care and consecration of the Servitors—were looked upon to provide hope through their words, teachings, and interpretations of the machines' wants, needs… desires.

But Fikrul saw another path—one that would later be mimicked and twisted by the techno-deviant Splicers in the Plaguelands of Earth while he and his explored their own darker interpretations of faith.

Fikrul is a Fanatic.

Scorned and abandoned.

Fikrul is all who strive to regain strength of self and purpose. He is a survivor. He is the outcast priest of the broken plains, and his sermon is death and all the glory that follows.

In Fikrul's eyes, and those of the outcasts who rallied to his philosophies, machines were not superior. They were not gods. They were tools. Instruments to be mastered and controlled and manipulated in service of Eliksni pride. None should grovel for Ether. None should have their honor bound to the whims of manufactured deities.

But the evolution of Fikrul's faith did not end there. If the machines—the very things that had regulated the whole of their existence—were tools, why not life itself? Why not death?

There are many tales of the time between Fikrul's fall and his rise again as spiritual leader of the Scorned Barons—his struggle to find strength as a battered Dreg, his journeys across the system to challenge his faith, his joining with the other outcasts who were scorned, and his eventual union with his "father." The only thing that matters, however, when confronting the dangers of Fikrul is this: He is a creature of faith.

His faith is the antithesis of all who stand in the Light. That faith has raised an army. That army will baptize all who challenge its purpose in an unending sea of death. They will never stop. They will never give in. Because they know they are right.

And everything you stand for is wrong.

A Gift of Madness

"The song of the grinding stone calls like pained sirens—shrill and uneven.
Its melody is a warning, yet still they come…
Adventurers. Bounty hunters. Scoundrels. And unwanted.
Here they find purpose.
Or hide from those worlds beyond.
Those polite lands, which 'heroes' strive to reclaim.
There is no reclamation here.
The Shore is ever-wild, and so shall it remain…
Ever the broken land where madness dwells and violence reigns."

—Excerpt from C.C. LaGrange's translations of
"Writings and Observations from the Tangled Shore: A Fallen Text"

The questions no one asks…

Was the Bomber always mad? Or was he driven to it? Was the madness a gift—or a curse?

Did the struggle for survival outside the structure and ritual of the House system crack his mind? The things he'd seen? Done? The Shore asks much of those who call it home. Most simply find their end through the harsh will of these harsh lands or by the hand of the hardened agents who stalk its fractured expanse—bandits, cutthroats, cannibals, Awoken patrols, Guardian "heroes."

There are a billion ways to die among the jagged wilds of the Tangled Shore. To challenge those odds is no small feat. To do so while maintaining self, rarer still.

However, isn't it also possible the Bomber was this all along? Mad. Deranged. Eager to inflict destruction. Lustful for the chaos and death to follow.

The Seeding of the Accretion Fields. The Bombing of the Origin Libraries. Kaniks's handiwork has been linked to numerous tragedies, both as a rogue enemy of the Reef and in league with his scorned brothers and sisters with whom he grew strong—with whom he found the purpose he once lacked.

These points—an examination on the birth of madness—I raise to address a lingering concern.

Seek the Awoken libraries. Speak to Cryptarchs with knowledge of the Reef… the Shore. Scour the records of the Bomber's deeds. Feel the pain of those who suffered the fire of his devastation. Remember the Fields. Weep at the unimaginable loss when the Libraries fell.

Allow yourself the comfort of knowing the sinister creature is now dead and gone by Guardian hand. But linger on victory's pride for only a short while, because the truth I seek to tell has yet to be revealed, and it is this…

The Mad Bomber is dead—Kaniks is no more. Yet the Shore remains ever untamed. Despite valiant effort. Despite your incredible strength.

And if the Shore remains tangled, its edges ever shifting, ever dire… Then who else may it drive to madness? First long-lost survivors of the fabled Golden Age, then stray Awoken and discarded Fallen…

Maybe next, the warriors of the Light. Guardians.

After all, more will surely come. And with more, however righteous you may be, the odds shift further in the Shore's favor. In the favor of madness.

And if not another, Guardian… why not you?

By Thy Tongue Be Damned

"Even here, the whispers persist.
Faint, but present."

—Excerpt from C.C. LaGrange's translations of
"Writings and Observations from the Tangled Shore: A Fallen Text"

A Dreg fell. Left to die. A forgotten pirate set on a path toward salvation. His crew had raided the Moon looking for Ether. They found only death. And then he was alone.

Hiraks, the small. Hiraks, the timid, the weak was lost to the depths of the Hellmouth. A solitary scavenger down among the hollows where dead things dwell. How he survived is a story untold, an impossible tale known only to Hiraks himself.

In that secret is his strength.

For poor, weak, pathetic Hiraks came out of that hell as something other. Still Fallen. Still alone. But changed by all he'd seen and learned—his mind opened, set adrift through the wonders of all the nightmares he had never imagined.

Some say he spent his time hidden in the shadows of that cruel land scouring the mysteries of the Worlds' Grave. Others suggest he peered into a hateful shrine and found truth in the unutterable horrors whispered from the abyss.

Truth is, only Hiraks knows. Truth as simple as it is puzzling: Yes. Yes, he did. Scour the Grave. Hear the whispers. Only then could all that followed transpire.

For a lowly Dreg to rise from their docking to stand as a Baron is rare enough, but that a Fallen of any stature could crack the layers of understanding that barricade the known universe from the ascendant plane is more than improbable. It was impossible.

Until it wasn't.

For Hiraks succeeded where so few have. He crafted his own throne world and began a monstrous quest to expand his knowledge, etching its harshest truths upon his enemies. And his work has progressed unchecked.

It is his name the children do not speak when sharing tales of the Haunting of Nemesis. It is his blood that Paladins and Corsairs alike wish to spill for the Slaughter at Gaspra.

Hiraks, the Twisted. Hiraks, Ascendant. The mindbender whose tongue is a weapon, whose experiments seek to unravel sanity and reshape imagination that his subjects may become other—tools of his vile bidding.

And so, the warnings spread...

When the Fallen who speaks in the language of the damned calls, do your best not to listen, for once his words take hold, your will shall fade, replaced by its antithesis.

And then, like that poor, weak, fallen Dreg... you too will know darkness.

You too will be alone.

Riddled with Lies

"Trust is your shield.
Trust is your weakness.
In the end, we all fall to betrayal."

—Excerpt from C.C. LaGrange's translations of
"Writings and Observations from the Tangled Shore: A Fallen Text"

A simple riddle for you to consider...

"Only truth can conquer lies. But what is truth? And in whose eyes?"

What then of the Butcher of Bamberga? What then of the Psyche Hordes' slayer? The Terminus of the Gray Legion? The Sliver of the Shadowed Veil? The Bandit of Old Bassa? The Dire Siren of Valian's Reprieve?

What then of so many who are one—a single scourge, responsible for many varied tragedies?

The Trickster. The liar. Silver-tongued Araskes, the Wit.

She who bartered with the Spider and nearly cost him his life. She who swindled a dozen bounty hunters that she alone may profit. So many tales of Araskes's sleight of hand and tongue and mind. The enemy who has won battles where no battle was fought. Who has killed more rivals than have ever risen to her challenge.

What is known and unknown? None can say. And the sly prankster would have it no other way.

Of all the Barons marked by scorn, it is Araskes to fear, for her greatest weapon is the dissolution of truth. She will give you certainty, only to reshuffle the deck. She will grant you your desire, only to reveal it is truly regret.

If this realm can allow for gods, then she may be the first among devils—unknowable, unpure. Her tongue will cut you down long before your body falls. If you don't believe—if you find yourself questioning the depths of her deceit—ask yourself a simple question:

Did you kill her? And if you did, did she die?

If the answer is yes, her trap is set.

If your answer is...

It's okay. You don't have to say it. Maybe you will survive out among these wild shores longer than most.

Though maybe not as long as you'd like.

Anguish, Ten-Fold

"Be weary of those who would do harm.
Yourself included.
Mind that you do not become undone.
For once infliction is tinged with joy, you are not but a beast.
And are we not more than that?
Do we not strive for better?"

—Excerpt from C.C. LaGrange's translations of
"Writings and Observations from the Tangled Shore: A Fallen Text"

It was Reksis Vahn who saw to the final days of the House of Wolves. With cold hatred, he hunted and slaughtered their Servitors until none remained, and thus a rabid House did fall.

But Reksis Vahn's rage was not sated, as the Wolves alone were not the architects of his fury—all Fallen who clung to the ritual of House politics were his enemy, total and complete.

It is told that he was starved as a young Dreg. He watched in agony as others grew strong while he and his closest brothers and sisters were kept low. They were unworthy, pathetic, unwanted. But Reksis was ever aware. He saw the lie of the Archon's worship—how Servitors were revered upon a pedestal of godhood as a means to control the masses.

Maybe there was a time when the Fallen theology was one with greater concerns. No more. The Houses fractured, at war with one another. Old graces long since neglected in favor of a more desperate purpose—survival.

While cast low, Reksis found strength in his growing hatred. Only when he found common disdain among those twisted outcasts who would call themselves Scorned—who wore their hated derision as a badge of honor—did Reksis also find an outlet for his anger. His new brothers and sisters saw great value in his unchecked aggression. They were all a bit mad in their own right. All a bit twisted.

But where others slipped toward insanity, Reksis's mind and intent were clear—the agony of a terrible death was his aim. The target of his wickedness, the very Servitors he had been denied. The very machines that sustained the Fallen.

He would tear and slice and rend their metal until their hissing deaths rang across the Shore, the Reef… the entire system. He would make all who do not stand with the Scorned Barons feel the anguish he once felt, tenfold.

And he would do so gleefully, watching the life drain from their eyes.

A Blind Eye Toward Tomorrow

"They who draw, mustn't always draw first.
For it is not speed that kills, but the eye—keen and sharp.
So, then, do not feel death.
See it. Know it.
And it shall manifest upon the trigger's embrace."

—Excerpt from C.C. LaGrange's translations of
"Writings and Observations from the Tangled Shore: A Fallen Text"

Pirrha, the Phantom. Pirrha, the Blind. The Fallen Baron with the all-seeing eye and the crack-shot. The Awoken link him to the legend, "The Ghost of Hellrise Canyon," believing it was Pirrha, and Pirrha alone, who haunted the winding depths, picking off intruders and holding off Corsair raiding parties as his fellow Barons planned their violent reign in the maze of caverns near the canyon's heart.

He was unseen during the Wolves uprising, but many credit him with the assassination of the Queen's palace guard. None can verify, but each fell to a single shot—clean, precise, fatal.

But how can a blind pirate who had been discarded and scorned by his House become the deadliest shot this side of Mars?

This is where the Barons' true strength hides. They are each a devil worthy of your hate, but together they are so much more. Not simply devils, but Hell itself—manifest, angry, and aggressive.

Rumors and legend merge to tell of the Machinist's expert hand, the Rifleman's cybernetic eye and a link between his sight and the tracking systems on his rifle.

What he sees, he hits.

What he hits, he kills.

There is evidence of Fallen giving themselves to technology. Becoming other—becoming more—as they marry their physical selves to enslaved mechanics. The mercenary Taniks is one example—more machine than Fallen now, an abomination in the eyes of traditional Fallen belief. The Splicers and their augmentation through SIVA—a twisted experiment brought low by the mighty hand of the heroes of Iron. Is Pirrha any different?

The Barons and Taniks and the Splicers are each and all individual dangers, driven by their own ambition. They are more likely to wage war with one another than see their commonality.

Yet are they not of a kind? Are they not evidence of something greater wending its way through the Fallen's dying culture?

Are they not the warning signs of a new terrible evolution?

One can only wonder—and hope—these horrid amalgamations of life and technology are simply outliers and not a promise of tomorrows yet to come.

The Ragged Valley Sprint

"Many are lost to the Shore's wayward ebb and flow.
The shifting mass gives and takes—pulls and tears.
The ground beneath ever uncertain, so tread carefully, as other dangers distract.
But death lingers, its grip loose but present.
Waiting to take hold.
Waiting to embrace all who walk these tangled lands."

—Excerpt from C.C. LaGrange's translations of
"Writings and Observations from the Tangled Shore: A Fallen Text"

The Ragged Valley is long and harsh and no valley at all. Not by traditional definition. Its hollow length runs between a series of lashed asteroids on the Shore's far western edge.

They call it a "valley" to be poetic, but in truth, it is simply the chaotic space between massive rocks that scrap and smash into one another in a violent dance. The distances from mass-to-mass ebb and flow without warning—a constant, deadly repositioning of the landscape. That ever-changing hollow is the Valley. Only the mad and desperate would dare run its length. With one exception…

Yaviks. The Rider.

The reason she made the run changes with the telling. You know she is neither mad nor desperate what with her skills on a Pike and killer determination. But the run itself—it's a legend as awe-inspiring as any Guardian's, save the fact Yaviks is a wicked beast and better off dead. The story goes…

She was running Ether… or making off with lost Golden Age tech. Some say Clovis Bray science. Others tell it was drivers from a forgotten Warmind. Or maybe she'd just dropped a Guardian and was running full-throttle from a fireteam set on revenge—a common theme this far out. Or was it pride? Did a Captain or a Kell or an Archon challenge her ability to ride? Did Fikrul? After all, their relationship is… complicated.

None of that matters. Not to me. Each version of the start is as interesting as the next. But the run itself? Her ride through the gnashing jaws of death?

Most Guardians who have heard it dismiss it. Don't want to give credit to one so infamous—the Scorned Baron with the blood on her hands, the loot in tow and her burners set to top speed—but she deserves it. Don't believe me. Ask Marcus Ren.

He wasn't there that day, but he'd heard tell and couldn't believe. So he made the run himself. Four goes. No dice. One resurrection. Four Sparrows busted to rubble.

Marcus Ren, the Sparrow Racing League champion and hero to speed junkies and race hounds City-wide, couldn't sprint that Valley. "Too random," he said. "Too chaotic. Can't read the rock one minute to the next. Can't read the angles."

But he tried again, and on the fifth go, he scraped through a narrow as the collision hit. He'd made it. The impossible was possible, though he refused to admit Yaviks could've done the same. Not that it mattered.

That Ren had come out alive proved it could be done, and if it could—why not Yaviks?

Not that Yaviks ever cared for validation. Not yours. Not Ren's. Not any Guardian's. Not any Fallen's. Not anyone's.

She took pride in recognition from her brother and sister Barons and no others.

Truth Tinkered

"Out here, they who craft their own fate see tomorrow, while they who depend on faith rarely make it through today."

—Excerpt from C.C. LaGrange's translations of
"Writings and Observations from the Tangled Shore: A Fallen Text"

If you had not heard of the Machinist before, know that others had. While her crimes may not live in infamy in the hearts of City-dwellers, the Reef and its Awoken know all too well her long reign of terror.

Elykris, the Bandit, they call her. Elykris, the Scourge. The Scorned Machinist—tinker-lord of a Houseless crew.

But should those names be new to your ears, there are others you trust who have felt the pain of her vile campaign.

Ask your Arach of the Machinist's deeds. Ask him about the Siege of Arran—the hijacked ship, its stolen contents and its Guardian protectors lost or captured at the hands of the scorned.

Speak to your Vanguard of the Solis Descent—more Guardians felled, and an armory stripped of its cache.

The lowly Dreg who challenged tradition only to be cast aside. The lowly Dreg who found her own strength in a troubling bond with forsaken kin. She grew strong as an outcast—grew mean. Then found her purpose with the guidance of a preacher of sorts and a new, more driven crew.

Now, then… the questions you must ask yourself…

Had you known of the Baron's deeds, had you heard tell of the Machinist's crimes—could you have changed the path tread from there to here? From yesterday to today?

Better yet… your Vanguard, your factions, your friends and allies—what all have they kept from you? If they spoke not of the Scorned Barons, if they issued no warning, is it because they simply did not see the full scale of the danger? Were they too distracted by wars within wars and interests of their own to issue the guidance needed for you to see the Shore for the threat it has always been? Perhaps given guidance that may well have saved countless lives?

Or at least one life in particular…

A Scorned Path

"Surviving is a whole lot easier when your enemies are dead."

—Excerpt from C.C. LaGrange's translations of
"Writings and Observations from the Tangled Shore: A Fallen Text"

It was Elykris, the Machinist, who'd begun hoarding the Servitors. And Reksis, the Hangman, who slaughtered them at every turn. Two allies driven by opposing forces—one science and the unmaking of faith, the other rage and its relentless push to destroy.

There had long been tension between the two, as Reksis had, more than once, slipped into the Machinist's workshop to inflict himself on the Servitors caged there.

Fikrul, the Fanatic—their spiritual leader and one-time Archon Priest—watched patiently as their rivalry grew. He saw strength in their ire. He saw fire and fury, but also more—a new path forward. One that could join their passions and drive them further—a whole stronger than its warring parts.

Fikrul waited, biding time as tensions rose and threatened to splinter the Barons' loyalties. Only when Elykris could take no more, on a night when she caught the Hangman prepared to slaughter her latest haul of lesser Servitors, did Fikrul step in.

Fikrul motioned to Elykris and said, "Bring me a Servitor." As Reksis hissed

with anticipation, she hesitated, but Fikrul was patient. "Where is your trust?"

Elykris released a Servitor from its bondage.

Fikrul motioned the Servitor closer, then turned to Elykris. "You have gathered many, Machinist. Hundreds. Maybe more. Our own supply—our life force fed by slaved mechanics." Elykris nodded to the Servitor as it inched closer to the Archon's open arms—welcoming the once revered orb as one would a child.

The other Barons began to bark, a rhythmic warriors' chant.

"For all the value in your work... it is not enough to feed ourselves." Fikrul hugged the Servitor. There was a tenderness to the embrace. A sorrow. "We must also starve our enemies, as you were once starved." With a blur, Fikrul's lower arms unsheathed and triggered a pair of polished, sparking Shock Blades. "As were we all."

The Servitor, still held with the clutches of the Archon's powerful upper arms, cried a shrill, digital wretch—pain mixed with confusion as the blades carved its outer shell and plunged deep into the core of its systems. Ether hissed and sprayed.

Fikrul released the machine's silent shell, and it clanged lifeless to the ground. He turned to Elykris. "Do you see?"

Elykris smiled. She was ever the brightest among them, though her focus could lose clarity when she became frenzied.

The Barons had long been trouble for the Awoken and Fallen of the Reef, but that trouble had been limited to hit-and-run tactics. What Fikrul had just presented was a new way.

Fikrul stepped to Reksis. "Do you see?" The brute barked in response, "Kill them all!"

Fikrul laughed. "Not 'all,' Hangman. Just the ones we do not need."

The Barons cheered as Fikrul continued, "Every Servitor—any Servitor—bound to a House is now a target. Until none remain but those upon whom we feed."

"We... are alike. Trapped in death...
a never-ending dance."

—Fikrul

Cayde-6 Reminisces
Fallen

Okay, okay, I'll tell the story about that one Fallen.

It didn't happen like that. We didn't, you know, do anything actively—no handshake, no icy stare of grudging mutual respect. I don't even know which hand you would shake. Do they shake hands? It must be complicated.

Anyway, it was like this. I was on the Moon. I cracked a Hive structure near Mare Imbrium, looking for a Shrine, and they just—swarmed. Ranks and ranks and ranks of Thrall, pouring out between the columns, but the columns were Knights, and all the shadows behind them rose up hissing sorcery.

Of course I ran.

I had a line of egress and while yes it was full of Thrall I had a backup too. I went upslope. Took cover in the shadow of a crashed Phaeton. Emptied my machine gun, ducked down to reload, and saw her at the other end of the hull, killing Thrall: a Fallen in Exile colors, bannered in the marks of a Baron, though the flags were claw-torn and stained with Hive ash. She was alone. I think she must have lost her crew.

I didn't really have time to shoot her and she didn't really have time to shoot me so we just went back to killing Hive. Knights pushed me out into the open and back up the range to a high stone saddle in the shadow of an old interferometry array. It was good ground so she came up there too.

For a while we just killed things which is hard to make interesting in a story so I'll pass it over.

At the end the Wizards came. I climbed the array to get an angle on them and she fell back to the base of the antennae where she broke her swords off in a Knight. I saw that happen and I don't know if I can tell you how I felt. She was another living thing with a mind I could understand and she hadn't howled at me or tried to eat my Ghost. I cheered when the Knight went down.

When I came down, empty on all guns, she was slumped against a bulkhead staring at me with all her tiny black eyes. Ether leaking out of her like smoke. The Knight hadn't died easily. Downslope the last Wizard moved like fire behind another line of Thrall.

I looked at her and wondered how many innocent human lives she'd ended on those broken blades.

She did the strangest thing then. Took the last shock pistol from her bandolier and threw it between us, as if to offer it. When I went to pick it up she tried to knife me, but she was slow, and when I broke her arms and opened her throat she didn't seem surprised.

To this day I wonder if she hated me, or wanted to make me kill her, or just felt she should spare me the choice.

I did kill a few Thrall with that pistol.

Misraaks

Book: The Dreaming City

The Vandal stoops as he exits the Galliot. All of his arms are bound behind his back, so he cannot shield his eyes from the bright sun. A breeze stirs his cloak. There is a cliff behind him and lush gardens ahead. His jailer would not grant him the honor of a quick death, so she must intend to torture him. She thinks he will yield like the flesh-lovers from House Judgment. She is wrong. Whatever indignities she can muster are nothing compared to what he deserves.

With his chin held high, he imagines shucking off his armor and laying all four of his arms in his Captain's hands. His Captain is his mother, and she will not dock him with a scythe. She will twist and tear his arms from his body like she is shucking a fine, fat crab for dinner, and he will be glad of the slow, sick cracks and crunches of his bones. He will be glad of the shame. Let him go limbless for the rest of his wasted life. Let the Ether-thirst shrivel him up like a yaviirsi fig.

"What do you think?" his jailer asks in a language he cannot understand. She steps up beside him and claps a hand on his shoulder. He flinches. She is nearly as tall as he is, and for a creature with no claws, her grip is strong and sure.

Together, they contemplate the gardens.

"It's all a bit much for my taste," she admits as he sneaks a furtive look at her.

Her bow is unstrung. There is only one arrow in her quiver.

She is stupid.

He whirls, trips her, and sprints for the cliff. She swears, recovers, and lunges after him. As he pitches himself off the edge, he thinks of his mother's shame and prays that she forgets him. Better that she never had a son than a weakling so easily captured by the enemy.

It is his bad luck that she catches his foot with one hand. His helmet slams into the rocky cliffside. A piece of his rebreather cracks off and disappears into the mist far below. He flails, but he cannot drag her down with him; somehow, she hauls him in like a fish. As soon as she has him on solid ground, she binds his ankles with the string of her bow.

"All right," she says, catching her breath. "All right." She chuckles, pats his shoulder fondly, and then pulls him upright like a sack of psakiks.

She takes a step back, brushing off her hands against the seat of her trousers. He glowers, the surliest psakiks sack this side of the Great Machine, hating her horrible, squared-off teeth and her blunt, stubby fingers. "Let's try this again, shall we?"

Drawing two fractal knives from sheaths on her thighs, she makes a perfect ireliis bow before him. Thunderstruck, he sits up straight. Stares.

"Not good?" she asks, and tries again.

Furious confusion takes him. This is some kind of trick. Blasphemous mockery. "Iirsoveks," he rumbles.

She shakes her head. "Nama." Sheathing one of her knives, she holds out her free hand with her fingers spread in supplication.

He draws his chin toward his throat with this fresh betrayal, narrowing his secondary eyes. It speaks!

Slowly, without breaking eye contact, she lays her other knife on the ground between them. The blade points toward her boots. He watches her every movement. How many secrets have the flesh-lovers betrayed, that this creature can make peace like a cringing drekh before his kel?

She taps two fingers against her cuirass. "Sjur," she says slowly, then she points at him.

Honor-bound even as he simmers in scandal, he replies, "Misraaks. Velask, Si-yu-riks."

"Mithrax," she repeats, then grins.

"Velask, Mithrax. And welcome! Let's have a look about, shall we?"

Lord of Wolves

By this right alone do I rule.

"Why did they call themselves Wolves?" the Hunter asks. "You guys don't have any wolves on your home world, do you?"

"Nama," the Captain replies. He has perched on a rusted-out Skiff. He scans the horizon, trying to remember the way to the crypt.

"So… Why, then? Most people haven't even seen one."

"Yeah," the Warlock chimes in. "I'd never even heard of wolves 'til I went to the Iron Temple."

The Captain cocks his head in a way that makes him look very like a squat, hulking owl. "Why Eliksni accept name 'Fallen'? Why Wolves accept name 'Wolves'? Why Misraaks is now," he grimaces as he mimes their accents, showing his serrated teeth, "Miff-racks?" He rises in one fluid motion and stands at his full height. "Why speak Guardian way instead Eliksni? Docked things do not word themselves."

He hops down, brushing past the Hunter and the Warlock with the rippling strength of a hunting tiger. "House of Wolves, they been Mraskilaasan. Gentle weavers. Come. I know the way now."

The Queenbreaker

Despite the Breakers' treachery,
Her Majesty still stands.

Three cloaked figures trek through a cave on a windswept asteroid. As they walk, they joke. They tell stories. They are a fireteam.

"After Cybele," the Warlock says, "the Wolves bowed. Some became the Queen's bodyguards. Then, Skolas—"

"Whoa, whoa, whoa. How? Why?" The Hunter frowns. "Why trust enemies with your life?" A pause. "No offense, buddy."

The Captain shrugs: none taken. "Eia. Strange to do. But Eliksni… we been breathe-always love for honor. New promise not unmake an old. Wolves would been follow Marakel forever if Skolas does not appear again."

The passage widens, and they find a hidden door veneered with amethyst. The Captain lays a hand on it, bows his head. The Hunter and the Warlock fall back respectfully. After a time, the Warlock ventures, "Mithrax?"

The Captain turns. "Wolves rebel. Now, Wolves extinct. This where-live mine-things scatter must end. I will Kell the mind-open Eliksni. No spider-tricks. No loyal-lies. Variisis truths. We fight for Great Machine together."

CHAPTER 9

Succession

"I assure you, what you are hearing of me are lies."

—Variks, the Loyal

Variks, the Loyal remembers an ancient time, and an ancient name: the House of Judgment, when grudges and status fights were worked out in a safe place. When the berserk and the vengeance-crazed were kept somewhere harmless, and there were fewer rivals to plot around.

The old Fallen ways align perfectly with the Queen's agenda. With the House of Wolves in disarray, the Queen needs muscle in the Reef. Guardians go where the treasure and the glory are, and an arena of champions is a wonderful place to earn both. Guardians in the Reef deter threats to the Queen and give the Awoken a chance to learn about their power and subvert their loyalty to the Traveler. And if, as the Queen worries, the Nine are scheming against her, then she needs a good excuse to clear out some of the most dangerous prizes in the Prison of Elders.

And the Prison of Elders is full of dangerous prizes. The Awoken have captured titanically dangerous specimens from everywhere in the inner solar system. These monstrous champions want to smash Guardian bone and Guardian alloy—and given the chance, they'll kill Guardians, rend their Ghosts, and snuff them out forever. Walk into the arena with a Fireteam you trust. And beware: the agents of the Nine are active in the Reef, and their curiosity is as limitless as it is inscrutable.

Risk death. Win glory and signs of Her Majesty's favor. But always remember that you are being watched, and tested.

Splinter of Bone

Deep in the heart of the Prison of Elders, Variks of House Judgment clutched a splinter of bone as he watched the solar system burn.

The facility had been outfitted over the years with massive sensor grids slaved to arrays spread across the Reef. They gave him a detailed analysis of the Red Legion's fury. The light from the monitors was the only illumination in the room as his arms flew across the controls.

Relaying warnings to Petra and the Awoken. He could already see the remainder of the Awoken fleet disappearing off his scopes, going into hiding.

Relaying warnings to the City, though he could see he was far too late. Their comms were gone. There was no one left to listen.

Relaying warnings to his people. With the end of the Houses, there were so few who would listen. But if he could save even a handful…

While his hands worked, his eyes remained fixed on the screens, watching death, destruction, and horror.

In his role working with the Guardians of the City, he'd pored over the distress signal from the Dantalion Exodus VI. Source GREENRAVEN had sent bursts of analysis to the Tower at least a dozen times since the days of the Taken War. But he'd never expected numbers of this magnitude.

With the systems of the Last City offline, he had no problem dialing sensors over the Wall. He'd been able to see with clarity the home of Humanity with a resolution where he could make out parks and lakes and marketplaces.

These same sensors let him watch, grinding the bone in his mechanical fist, as people died. As the Great Machine was yoked, as the Guardians… fell.

Scrambling, he alerted the Crows… but something went wrong. The network had fallen dark—each and every Crow offline. All, that is, save for one. Through a garbled image he saw a hand, an Awoken hand, but it almost immediately fell to static. He wanted to care. He wanted to feel something for them. What dominated his thoughts, though—what made a ticking noise emanate deep in his voice synth—was the growing fear that the Queen's plan had failed.

He sat back in his chair. Thinking.

The Prison of Elders orbited far enough away from the core Awoken outposts, and thus far enough away from the Cabal's Phalanx, that it might come out of this unscathed. Nonetheless, he initiated lockdown procedures, prepared for the worst.

A comm ping. Confirmation: Petra Venj and the limited forces at her command evacuated what settlements they could and disappeared into the nooks and crannies of the Reef. She would be unable to send help to the Prison.

First House Judgment, then House Wolves. Then Kell Mara Sov. Now he could feel the rest of his adopted people slipping away from him.

With one of his mechanical arms, he crushed the splinter of bone to dust.

Less Is More

Variks watched Petra's Corsairs march their latest prize into the cellblock: a gaggle of Ether-starved Dregs bearing the mark of the Scorned Barons. Nearby, Petra drummed her fingers along the hilt of her knife; her eyes glinted with envy.

She held onto this prison as if it was the last thing she could control. Perhaps it was. Between the scattered remnants of the Red Legion and the Scorned Barons running rampant through the Reef, the Awoken had little left to call their own.

Variks sighed. Only a true Kell understood that survival was not a game of waiting. And Petra Venj, for all her military prowess, was no Kell.

"In a world without Kells, Dreg strength will breed nothing but chaos." Variks whispered to himself the old Rain proverb, wishing for the return of the decisive days of his Queen. His Kell.

"What did you say?" Petra asked without looking at him.

"Chaos," he replied. "These Dregs breed chaos."

Petra scoffed. "They're Fallen. And where there's Fallen, there will inevitably be Guardians." She turned on her heel and walked away. "I leave you to your Judgment, Variks. Locate the hole in which these Scorned Barons cower." She stopped. Turned back to him. "Might want to up your rations. You're looking a bit... gaunt."

She smiled, patted him on the back, and continued on her way.

He watched her go. If his anatomy allowed for it, he would have smiled in kind. Hers was a heart always in the right place... even if the outcome of her decisions was less than ideal. She did not, however, fully appreciate the threat these "Scorned" Barons posed. He had tried to warn her when they were just seven Dregs and a heretical Archon. Now their terror was spreading throughout the Reef with more and more Fallen answering the Barons' anarchistic call.

She was right about one thing though: He could stand to increase his intake. The thought of it made Variks thirsty for the flow. Like all of his kind since the appearance of the Red Legion, he had been forced to ration his intake. He'd never felt so weak, so close to death. But he would survive as he always had.

Variks knew the time would inevitably come when he would have to survive on his own.

Roll Call

After the Taken War, the Scorned Barons banded together in a time of weakness to become strong, to prey on anyone and anything that practiced the old Eliksni ways. They began with the one thing their people needed to survive: Ether. In a way, the Barons had become heads of a new House, priests in their own rites, and arbiters of their own trials.

The terror they unleashed had almost grown as powerful as any Kell. These heathens were not Eliksni; they were more "Fallen" than any of their brethren. They were everything Judgment had sought to purge before the Whirlwind—and now, they sat rotting deep in the Prison of Elders. Cayde and his "Six" had done good by their word.

Variks's staff tapped lightly on the floorplates, and chuckling noises emanated from his throat. He hobbled past their cells as the Servitors hummed to life.

Feeding time.

He saw hatred in every cell he passed. Bathed in the light of flowing Ether, their eyes carved at his flesh, saw him docked a thousand times more.

Yaviks, the Rider, the Untamed. She and her crew spread terror and disease with their noxious pikes.

Elykris, the Machinist. She used stolen Cabal telemetry and gravity traps to sabotage vessels, relieve them of their cargo, and haul the hulks back to their own shipyard chop shops.

Pirrha the Blind, the Ghost of Hellrise Canyon, who haunted the Baron's territory with phantom decoys and ended all trespassers from the shadows.

Reksis Vahn, the Godslayer, the Hangman. He had secreted away the Ether stores of his victims and driven the Barons and their followers into a frenzy with that tainted feast.

Arakses, the Wit. The Traitor. The Trickster. A mastermind. A liar, thief, and backstabber.

Kaniks Two-Finger, the Mad Bomber. The dangers of the Reef had multiplied a hundred-fold with his mines hidden on every rock and dusty corner of the belt.

And the most disgusting of them all, Hiraks, the Mindbender. This one found in the Hive a way to infect the minds of the Eliksni.

Only one was missing.

Fikrul. The Heretic. The Fanatic. One Variks once dared to call friend, back when the Archon tended to Kaliks Prime.

Before his betrayal. He hoped the Fanatic was dead; Cayde assured that he was. And what was Cayde-6 if not reliable?

Laughing, burbling to himself, Variks shut off the lights in the hallway. And the Barons were plunged once again into darkness.

Job Undone

In the Prison of Elders' security hub, Variks brooded.

When the Great Machine woke, he had been sure he felt something deep within him stir. He had hoped it would give him answers, power, anything. All it did was remind him how far he had fallen.

He slammed a fist on his console, watching the denizens of the prison claw at their cell walls. No, not nothing. Worse than nothing. Now he had doubt.

His goal had always ever been a simple one. The banner of House Judgment, the calling to which he had been born. Keep his people together.

With the Light now streaming across the system and nothing to show for it—no Queen, no Eris or Osiris, and no sign the Great Machine remembered the Eliksni—what was there to look forward to? Base survival. One day after the other. Living just because he still drew breath. And where was the Dreg strength in that? What was the...

"Variks." Petra burst through the comms. "A Legion Harvester has been intercepted at bearing 189. Capture teams are inbound. Survivors for the arena. Prepare to receive."

Petra Venj was all that was left for him here, and despite himself, he nodded at the sound of her voice. He had but one ally left, after all.

He keyed the comms. "Yes, yes, yes. Bay 41. Bring them in, will meet team. Will make room for new... guests." His vocal synth burbled, needing tuning.

"Copy that." She was gone.

He picked up his staff from where it leaned against the wall and began the long walk to the bay. Mulling his options, his information. His secrets.

Secrets had protected the House of Judgment. The more knowledge one could obfuscate, the more significant one became. Secrets bred possibility. Secrets bred... sway.

But Judgment, true Judgment, required hierarchy. And Eliksni hierarchy died with the fall of the Houses. The Guardians had picked them apart, Kell by Kell, Prime by Prime. Now, there was all but nothing left of his culture—only pirates and scavengers and lone wolves like the days before the Edge Wars. No trust, no honor, no way to be... necessary.

Yet one final hope among the Eliksni still thrived. Craask, Kell of Kings. The Kings understood Judgment, for together they ended the Edge Wars in their people's golden age. Craask. His last hope to see his dreams of a united Eliksni made manifest. He must make contact.

And so he hired a bounty hunter named Groks to find Craask and remind them of their need for one another. Groks is emblematic of all that Variks despises in his people—gluttonous, proud, and in it only for himself. When they spoke, Groks made Variks pay with a litany of insults.

Variks the Slip. Variks the Beggar. Variks the Kell-Maker. But it was all for show. Groks would work; and it came for a mere four bales of Etheric Helix and a promise to keep him free of the Prison of Elders. The deal struck, Groks burst out in hysterical laughter.

"Ha! Consider job done, Slip!" Groks spoke in a low form of Eliksni, the only reason Variks employed him. "You have grown desperate with your 'Kell' gone. Have you not heard?"

Variks sighed.

"King Kell is gone, Kell-Maker. Dead at the hands of that insane Archon, Fikrul, and some Awoken vagabond he calls 'Father.' What remains of the Kings huddles now in the dead zones of Earth, under the shadow of the Great Machine's Shard. I expect my four bales in—"

Variks killed the feed. The last link in the great Eliksni chain was broken. If there were any who called themselves Kell out there, they would not know Variks, Judgment, or the laws that governed the Houses. The scattered children of the Whirlwind were dead.

But... Fikrul survived Cayde and his Six? Groks was a lot of things, but he was not a liar. If Fikrul was alive and strong enough to kill Craask... And who was this Awoken vagabond of which Groks spoke? His mind reeled. So long as Fikrul lived, the Reef was not safe. He scrambled through his comm channels, searching for the right connection.

"Master Cayde. Variks requests to meet you regarding your deal with Petra, a job undone."

Some Kind of Luck

Variks hid beneath a bannerless cloak as he descended into Spider's lair. To wear the Judgment sigil in the Tangled Shore would be to invite death. Even with the Spider's blessing to pass, he would have been picked clean and docked two times over.

The hedonistic sounds of Spider's Palace scraped against him. Shouts of victory and defeat reminded Variks of the worst of the Eliksni. His peoples' inherent need for superiority reduced to gambling for trinkets and gems.

Variks searched the crowd, hunched down low. Just another Vandal. In the corner, the unmistakable crowd that surrounded the Hunter Vanguard when he was outside the City.

He worked his way through the onlookers to take up position alongside Cayde. The Hunter noticed him, he was sure, but said nothing. Variks, for his part, was silent. Watched as he lost a few thousand Glimmer and a sidearm to one of Spider's bodyguards.

Cayde spun a knife in his right hand and sighed dramatically. "If we're going to talk, you're going to buy me a drink."

They found a quiet place at the end of the room. Cayde settled back in the booth. Waiting.

"You do great service to Reef, yes?" Variks worked hard to keep his very recognizable voice down. It would be a shame for his vocal synth to malfunction and blare out across the room now. "Capture Barons. Criminals. For Awoken. For Petra."

Cayde took a belt and set the glass down on the table, empty. Something hard around his eyes. Amazing how expressive Exos could be. "Get to the point, Variks."

"Fikrul. The last Scorned Baron. He lives."

Cayde's horn cut an arc through the air as he shook his head, twice, definitive. "Trust me. He's dead. Put a hot one right through here." He poked Variks right in the center of his chest.

"Seen on Earth. I have knowledge. I have information. You know Eliksni have ways. Like Mithrax? Like Taniks?" The warden realized his error as soon as the name was out of his mouth.

"Don't you EVER mention the name Taniks around me, got it? Not unless you want to lose your last two real arms. We're done. Get. You're bad luck." The Hunter stood, made to leave. Variks reached out and grabbed the Vanguard by the arm with one of his mechanic hands.

"I am sorry. I spoke poorly. Please. Listen."

Cayde shrugged off the arm and stood, towering over the Fallen for once.

Variks sat up straighter in the booth. "Take me to Zavala." The Titan Vanguard's name was a punctuated, flowing stutter in his mouth. "I have information. He will like what I say. You for bringing me to him."

Cayde blinked. "You want me to take you to the City? No way, bug. Not in a million…"

With a thud, Variks dropped the hand cannon he'd been hiding in his cloak on the table: a dull brown, bristles out the top, Ethertech trigger and muzzle assembly. Cayde's eyebrows went up in surprise.

"A gift of trust. Memento of the Reef. Upgraded, yes? Very deadly."

The Hunter Vanguard tried to hide his excitement. "Is. Uh. Is that the last one? I haven't seen one of those in…"

"One of the last. Not many left." Variks's voice was even, calm.

Cayde snatched the weapon from the table. Checked the sights, spun it in his hand for a moment, feeling the weight. Grunted, satisfied. Nodded.

"Like I said: bad luck. C'mon. You can ride with me."

Overestimation

Variks had never seen the Vanguard Commander in person before. The images he'd seen were either candid shots from agents or images from co-opted surveillance that didn't reveal the man's true stature. Most of Zavala's "bulk," he realized, was the armor. He was a lean man, in reality. Taut muscle and sinew.

But as Variks stood before him, he realized Zavala's poise and confidence, along with his Light, controlled the space around him. Lent him an air of authority Variks had not felt since standing in the presence of Mara Sov herself. Even Cayde, of all people, seemed somehow different in the orbit of this man.

Fascinating.

Behind the Light and the poise, Variks could see where the great Zavala's strength ended and anxiety began. That was where Variks needed to meet him and prove his worth.

"Vanguard Commander Zavala." Variks dropped to his knees and extended his hands palms up on the ground, sure to keep eye contact. A Judgment gesture meant to acknowledge that a dominant force was present.

Cayde snickered behind him, but said nothing.

"Variks came to offer assistance. To help the Vanguard. The Guardians, who have helped the Reef."

Zavala stared Variks down. The Judgment scribe saw much in that moment. Fortitude. Intensity. Desperation.

"On your feet, Variks." Zavala was quite used to giving commands and having them followed. Variks did as he was commanded. "What do you want?"

"A future for the Reef." Zavala eyes were searching. Variks croaked and continued. "Reefborn are close to doom, Zavala the Awoken. Fallen, Taken, Red Legion. All carve at the Reef. All claim its flesh."

"I made my offer to Petra after the war." His voice was gruff, but not uncaring. "She made her choice. Are you saying something has changed?

"I say this, Commander." Variks burbled. "And I have so much more to say to a true leader such as you."

Unknown Space

The light seemed to dance in blue over the horizon of unknown space, but all else was black.

Tendrils seemed to grow with the light. Where they were reaching from or stretching toward, he could not comprehend. Fear gripped Variks's mind. The paths before him were vast, uncertain. And for the first time in his life, he could sense Judgment turned inward.

"Your will must remain your own," he told himself. "You are the last Eliksni of House Judgment. The destiny of your people is in your hands. You will save them. You will stand for the Fallen."

YOU WALK AMONG THEM, BECAUSE YOU HAVE FAILED.

The voice, soft and yet so strong, echoed around him in the space. Through him, like he was a string on an instrument.

"I walk among the children of Earth and the blessed of the Great Machine, the one they call Traveler, because they have been chosen."

FOR YOU THE GREAT MACHINE IS A DARK MIRROR.

Variks felt cold unlike he had ever known. Unbidden, memories rushed past him. All he could do was hang on as the last days of the Eliksni played out in his mind.

He and his fellow scribes passing Judgment in their soft, furred robes. Then the Whirlwind, the Elders torn apart, the pillaging of the House. Variks, kneeling before a window, staring up at the Great Machine. Watching it vanish. The long journey in the darkness.

His flight to run with the Wolves, his pleas to Skolas. The pact with Fikrul to sever Kaliks Prime and secret it away. The Prime vanishing… And again Fikrul, on the horizon, preparing to give the Fallen what they so rightfully deserve…

THERE IS ONLY ONE PATH LEFT FOR YOU HERE, IN A PLACE WHERE EVERYTHING DIES…

…AND BEGINS ANEW.

With that, a new power burned, affording him the strength to rise again. Judgment cast—

The screaming pulse of the prison alarms stirred Variks awake.

On the comms, he heard Petra's voice. Cayde had returned.

Two Cells

Petra called for not one, but two cells. Variks finished his Ether, considering. Perhaps Cayde had finally found Fikrul—and for that, Variks would need every drop of strength he could muster.

His strides were long and slow as he allowed the Ether to course through him, his posture growing taller and more commanding with each step. At the top of the maxsec wing, his hands flew over the controls. He prepared the two empty cells and ordered extraction Servitors into place, all the while reveling in the thought of the judgment of Fikrul. Finished, he stepped back and waited.

Snarling, yelling, the prisoners entered the wing. One, an Eliksni, Petra shoved hard into one of the two cryo-cells. The Fallen landed, weak, and Petra sealed the cell door.

Variks was all too pleased to see the hulking, disgraced Fikrul—the lifeline of the Scorned Barons, his once trusted co-conspirator and great betrayer—seething as the extraction Servitors whirred to life, sapping the heretical Archon of his precious Ether. Variks and Fikrul looked deep into one another's eyes, centuries of history passing between them in the space of a heartbeat.

Fikrul laughed.

Unnerved, Variks stepped away as Cayde dragged a ragged, humanoid figure—head bagged, face unseen. Cayde unceremoniously tore off the hood and tossed the humanoid—an Awoken man—into the open cell.

"And stay there!" Cayde said. His joke fell flat.

On hands and knees, the stranger looked up at his captors to reveal a familiar mess of crow-black hair, blue skin, and piercing yellow eyes.

"Variks…"

It was the face of Uldren Sov—brother to the Queen, prince of the Awoken, and heir to the Reef.

Reacquaintance

"Your Grace…" Variks couldn't help but use the title. Like a reflex.

As he looked into the prince's eyes, he saw a fleeting shadow of darkness dance across their normal ethereal golden glow. Variks looked back to Petra.

"Petra Venj… I—I do not understand."

"I know. It's… Something's wrong with him, Variks. He's… mad. Lock him down—lock down the entire cellblock. No one in but you or me. Speak of this to no one. As far as the system is concerned, Uldren Sov died over Saturn."

Variks looked to Cayde for answers, but the Exo just threw up his hands in defense.

"Don't look at me. Prince Whiny Face and Fikrul were thick as thieves when we found them. Took all I had in me *not* to shoot the both of them."

Petra nodded toward the now royal cell, and Variks, with only a hint of hesitation, sealed the hatch, locking Prince Uldren in.

"Now, Variks," Cayde said, smooth as ever, "you let me know if Fikrul here ever comes up to the arena. He and I have a conversation to finish."

"Of course. Of course." Variks noticed Petra's gaze lingered a little too long on the prince's cell. He could see she was troubled, even ashamed. Petra saw him watching and composed herself, back straight, all Wrath. She met his eyes. He could still see her trouble, her shame.

"Variks. My friend." Was that tenderness Variks heard in Petra's voice? "He is changed. His eyes…" She stopped herself. Reset. "If he speaks, don't listen. He speaks lies. Terrible lies." And with that, she walked away, Cayde close behind. The doors to the cellblock slammed shut behind them.

Variks stood there for a long, long time. For the first time in his life, he didn't know what the next step should be.

Petra Venj and Uldren Sov had long admired one another; there was an easiness about them when they were together, and a deep if unspoken affection. When the two of them joined forces in the field of battle, they were quick, effective, and dangerous. Theirs was a dance of death, and woe to the foe who met them in open combat.

Variks wondered for what crimes Petra would have Uldren judged. As he reopened the prince's cell, he wondered if Petra would have Variks himself judged.

Variks knelt before Uldren. "We thought you dead. But you are in my care now, yes?" His arms carefully brushed at the Awoken man, probing but gentle.

Uldren blinked and looked toward him—or rather, his golden eyes looked beyond him. Variks looked over his shoulder, just to check. Of course, no one was there.

"Sister…" Uldren croaked through dried, cracked lips. "What's to become of us now?"

Revolution

The explosion of Servitors snapped Variks away from the pull of the prince's words. He tried to move quickly, but one of his toes caught awkwardly on the grated catwalk, and he stumbled to the floor. He lifted his head to see the extraction Servitors lying shattered and lifeless, hissing as Ether evaporate wafted into the air.

Variks rose, moving cautiously, slowly, uncertain who or what might be loose. He checked every seal of Fikrul's cell, then gathered enough courage to peer into the porthole.

Fikrul was unaffected. If anything, he looked stronger than he did before. He stood there, glaring, a devilish grin plastered across his face. "Does it find my Ether… bitter?" he growled.

Indeed, Variks could see that something was wrong with this Ether. It was darker, tainted with something he could not identify. He tightened the seals of his mask as he examined the Servitors' remains, fearing whatever they pulled from Fikrul could be toxic. He moved through the fog-like gas as if it was water. It didn't dissipate like traditional Ether; it lingered, heavy and opaque.

Variks stepped back up to Fikrul's cell. Activated the transmission mic.

"Fikrul, asaalii akisoriks," he seethed, using the High Speak of Judgment, hoping that Fikrul might still respect the oldest law.

"Ah, Variks. You cling to Judgment like Rain clung to lies." Fikrul spat his words the way the Houseless would.

"You are Houseless. You are filth. Is this what you've done with Kaliks, served the last Prime to the Taken? Is that the blood you now breathe?"

"Ha! You still believe I have Kaliks. Fool. Kaliks abandoned us. But my Ether… It's true Fikrul is no longer enslaved to the machines' Ether. By the grace of the Awoken Father, I have evolved."

Variks looked back to the prince's cell, still open. The Awoken Father…

Variks ambled back to the prince. With each step, he heard more clearly. He saw Uldren sitting up now, nodding, listening, peering into the shadows at something unseen. If ever there was a picture of malevolent insanity, this was it.

The prince spoke.

"Yes, Sister. I see it now. The army of the reviled that you promised me…"

The Spark

Variks, ever the Loyal, did as Petra commanded: Access to the lowest cellblock was reserved strictly to the Warden and the Regent-Commander. Unfortunately, this meant that every menial operational task was left to him. Meal distribution. Waste disposal. Between the eight Barons and the Awoken prince, his new chores left him little time for Judgment.

Thrice per day, he visited the block. And thrice per day, he had to manufacture excuses to the local Corsair detachment for why the lowest level of the prison was now off limits. Rumors swirled. It was not unknown that Petra and Cayde-6 had smuggled some unknown high-value prisoner—a humanoid prisoner no less, a first for the Prison of Elders if the rumors were true. But Variks assured anyone with the gumption to ask that his Judgment of the Scorned Barons was a sensitive process to be conducted in private.

Petra herself did not help extinguish the scuttle. She was less than adept at the art of secrecy, and everyone knew it. She responded to any bold queries with a stern, "It is none of your concern," which itself was tantamount to a validation that some version of the rumors was true. If only she'd found joy in her Techeun training; if only she'd learned more from the Queen.

Each time Variks performed his rounds, he asked himself what loyalty—if any—he owed to the prince. And each time, he stopped short when he bore witness to the prince's… ramblings. Today was no different. There Uldren sat, elbows atop knees, staring into the same dark corner of the cell, face concealed by his long, black hair, seemingly communing with nothing.

"I see now… Yes, that's good, so good."

More listening; more nodding.

"Then that's what we shall do. And look, Sister, he is already here."

Uldren fell into silence, visibly relaxing. After a moment, he looked back over his shoulder and through the porthole to meet Variks's eyes.

"Your Grace," Variks burbled.

"Variks the Loyal." Uldren smirked. "Variks the Spark. Did you have something to say to me, or are you content to play the spying crow?" And there it was again—that fleeting pass of inky darkness that momentarily snuffs the glow of Uldren's eyes. So Variks said nothing. Whether frozen in terror or simply at a loss for words, he could not say.

Uldren leaned in, placed a finger against his lips, and spoke low: "I have a secret for you, Variks. I know you want to hear it."

Variks answered with a single, drawn out, and ever-so-slight nod.

"Your Kell lives," Uldren whispered. He leaned in a little closer and asked the one question Variks had never been able to answer: "Do you know where your TRUE loyalty lies, Variks?"

Uldren didn't wait for a response. His eyes almost immediately darted over his shoulder, toward the shadowy corner that has become his obsession.

"Of course we can trust him, dear Sister. He is the most loyal…"

Chain of Souls

Variks admired his masterpiece, the improvised Servitor chain that would finally reveal the secrets of his fanatical former friend.

Unfortunately, Fikrul refused talk of the past, would speak only of the future. Or of Uldren, his Awoken "father," who snatched him from the edge of death and awakened within him a power never before seen in the Eliksni. A power over death itself. A power to remake their people and thrive in a universe of Light and Dark that had both forsaken them and left them scorned.

Variks knew these feelings all too well. It was here, in the deepest catacombs of the Prison of the Elders, where he thrived, where he worked to rebuild the Eliksni. This was his home now, this workspace where he was free to explore the "potential" of the prison's inmates for future leverage. The emerald marrow worm-food of the Hive, the prismatic viruses of the Vex, Psion Flayer wavelengths—each of these secrets had been wrested free within these dank halls, traded among his networks for more secrets, or harnessed into weapons for the Awoken.

But the secrets of Fikrul's... mutation... eluded him. The power within was obvious. Scattered about the floor was the evidence of its potency—as well as too many nights of failure: wrecked sentry Servitors, dozens of deflated Dregs, all

pulled from the upper cellblocks to act as his "assistants." Whatever this cold unnatural cocktail was that coursed through Fikrul, it could not be transferred or ingested like the Ether his people needed to sustain their wretched lives.

Variks was all too ready to give up, send Fikrul into the arena to face Cayde-6, and put an end to the legacy of the Scorned Barons—until one day, during Variks's rounds, Uldren spoke to him unprompted. There was a lucidity in the discarded prince's eyes, a clarity that didn't exist even before he disappeared over Saturn's rings. Uldren gave Variks a... fresh perspective.

And so, the chain. It was a dangerous gamble, mingling Fikrul's polluted lifeblood with traditional Ether. These Servitors held seventy percent of Variks's own Ether reserves. If this failed... well, it wouldn't be the first time Variks had risked everything and lost.

Variks pulled the lever.

The hum of the Servitor chain crescendoed, but all he heard was the lingering echo of Uldren's poisonous question: Do you know where your true loyalty lies, Variks?

But if it worked—perhaps Fikrul could be cured. Perhaps—if what Variks suspected was true, and Fikrul's corruption was related to the Prince's affliction—Uldren could be cured, too.

Variks had said as much to Petra, but she'd refused to listen.

"You will not experiment on the Prince."

"Our Prince is ill. To keep him here… hide him from Awoken eyes… not right. Not right."

"I've made my decision, Variks."

Variks's fingers flexed. "Petra, the Loyal," he sneered. "Perhaps the murmurs of Kamala Rior are true, yes?"

Petra glowered. "I will handle Uldren. You will not touch him."

She'd turned sharply on her heel and strode out. Variks hadn't seen her since.

He devoted all his time to the Servitor chain—and to his private thoughts.

Where Loyalty Lies

Variks's experiment succeeded, but not how he expected.

Ingestion of the Etheric concoction still resulted in Fallen death; it was not, by any means, a life-sustaining substance. It was, however, a life-GIVING substance. Though the dark Ether lingered like a heavy fog, it also seemed to reach out toward empty vessels. In this case, it found the dead Dregs that littered his floor. It slipped inside the corpses like a slow inhalation, inflating them, stretching them to the point of boils and bursting, pulling them to their feet. The dark Ether gave these lifeless Dregs… new life.

They seethed. Their breathing was steady, but hard and fast. They rumbled as if volcanoes lived inside their chests. A black fire rose from their skin as they burned this dark Ether like a jet engine burns its fuel. What Variks really saw before him was hate-fueled rage incarnate and the beginning of another Whirlwind. They were no longer just Fallen. Fikrul called them his Scorn.

Behind him, Fikrul laughed and laughed and laughed until—he abruptly stopped. At that exact moment, the Scorn dropped to the floor, dead once more.

"Your scribes, your Kells, your Houses— they will all soon be forgotten, like the Elders and the Skaith before them," Fikrul growled in Variks's precious High

Speak of Judgment. This drew Variks closer, face to face through the cell's porthole.

Fikrul turned his ear upward, listening. Brought his attention back to Variks. "Father says…" The pause hung heavy in the air. "Father says… You know where your true loyalty lies."

The Fanatic stepped back from the porthole and waited.

Loyalty. True loyalty.

He expected a memory of Mara to appear in his mind. But instead—

Instead he found himself thinking about the prophecies of House Rain.

Kell of Kells.

Days later, Variks performed his duties for the last time. He visited central control. Ran a test sim on the security systems, made some adjustments based on the results. Revised and signed off on the daily roster rotations. Finally, he had a private conversation with the prison's sole remaining High Servitor: The Prison of Elders would not go without a warden.

He did not speak to Petra.

By the end of that day, the Prison of Elders descended into chaos.

"Your time WILL come, Variks."

Uldren sits in his favorite spot, gazing in

his favorite direction. "She told me so. She has but one last wish of you."

"No, your grace." Variks's voice was gravelly with emotion. "It is I who has one last service for you."

Variks left before he could change his mind.

A klaxon blared. The voice of the prison's High Servitor echoed over the loudspeakers—in Variks's voice. "Security systems malfunction. Emergency shutdown and reboot commencing."

The place dropped momentarily into darkness, but emergency lighting quickly illuminated the cellblock. All around him, alarms sounded, warning lights flashed, pneumatics hissed, and cryogenic fluids evaporated to fog as the cryo-cells lining this cellblock began to open.

Variks moved as quickly as he could toward the exit, not bothering to look back, for he knew what he'd see.

The Scorned Barons and Prince Uldren were free.

As was every single resident of the Prison of Elders.

Variks slipped out, under cover of prison anarchy, through the same secret passage in which Petra and Cayde had smuggled Prince Uldren. There, a ship waited, loaded with the Prison's Ether stores.

As he walked, he made two recordings to be sent out by the Prison's relays once he was away. For the first, he disabled his voice

synth and began, in the deep resonance of High Speak, to give commands.

He didn't know how many would answer Judgment's call. But he had to try.

For the second, he turned his voice synth back on. "They call me betrayer. I who was most loyal. They do not think I hear the words. Bug. Insect." He paused. "Fallen."

Up, long strides, fast now, along the ramp into the ship. Toward the bridge. A Vandal in Wolf colors saluted him as he passed.

"I hear the words. House of Judgement always hears. No choice. To keep the Houses together." He paused again, as he reached the bridge of his ship. "Judgment always hears."

"The Great Machine stood in Judgment. Eliksni fell to fighting. Fell to hate." Emotion caught in his voice. "Cannot stomach this hate." As he spoke, the ship's engines rumbled to life. On the screens, Variks could see explosions resonating through the Prison. His former charges running rampant. His ship passed through the bay's barrier and began to move off.

"Nowhere else to go. No one else to be, here." He drew himself up to his full height. "And so I become Variks, the Kell. House Judgment envoy to the Eliksni people."

"No choice." He repeated, chuckling deep in his throat. His voice was calm. "Eliksni must rise... yes?"

TO EVERYONE WHO INSPIRED US, WHO SHARED OUR DREAM,
AND WHO WALKED WITH US ON THIS INCREDIBLE JOURNEY
—TO EVERY MEMBER OF THIS BRILLIANT COMMUNITY—
THANK YOU FOR BEING THE MOST IMPORTANT CHARACTERS
IN THE WORLDS WE BUILD.

DESTINY GRIMOIRE ANTHOLOGY, VOLUME II: FALLEN KINGDOMS

Based and built on the inspiring work of the talented individuals at Bungie—too numerous to note—who have each contributed to these words in their own unique and important ways.

Bungie

Contributing Writers

Seth Dickinson:
vi-vii, xi, xii, 19, 26-31, 33, 37, 40, 43, 48-49, 50, 55-56, 62, 63, 72, 76-77, 78-79, 84, 86-87, 132-133

Jonathan Goff:
19, 22-23, 26-31, 33, 60, 64, 69, 80, 89, 98, 114-128

Ted Kosmatka:
96-97

Eric Raab:
ix, 5, 14-15, 24, 26-31, 33, 65, 73, 81-83, 143-145, 148-162

Christine Feraday:
58-59

Jill Scharr:
7-8, 38-39, 51-54, 71, 107, 111, 112, 113, 143-145, 148-162

Mallory Schleif:
21, 134-135, 138, 139, 143-145, 148-162

Chris Schlerf:
90

Christine Thompson:
14-15, 17, 19, 91, 100

Jonathan To:
11-12, 98, 101-105

Michael Zenke:
9-10, 93, 98, 99, 143-145, 148-162

Bungie

Editor and Design:
Lorraine McLees

Art Direction and Cover Design:
Garrett Morlan

Illustrations:
Piotr Jabłoński

Additional art:
Sung Choi
Joseph Cross
Ryan DeMita
Dima Goryainov
Isaac Hannaford
Jaime Jones
Kekai Kotaki
Adrian Majkrzak

Graphic Design:
Zoë Brookes
Tim Hernandez

Franchise Direction:
Christopher Barrett
Luke Smith

Narrative Director:
Sam Strachman

Grimoire Curator and Editor:
Eric Raab

Additional Curation/Editorial:
Jason Harris
Christine Thompson

Lore Curation and Advisor:
Matt Jones

Layout:
Keith Lowe

Production:
Devon Detbrenner
Chris Hausermann

Copy Editor:
Stacey Janssen

Legal:
Aaron Kornblum
Marjorie Martin

Director, Consumer Products:
Katie Lennox

Creative Director, Global Brand:
James McQuillan

Blizzard Entertainment

Production:
Alix Nicholaeff
Derek Rosenberg

Director, Consumer Products Publishing:
Byron Parnell

TITAN BOOKS

A division of Titan Publishing Group Ltd
144 Southwark Street
London SE1 0UP
www.titanbooks.com

Find us on Facebook: www.facebook.com/titanbooks
Follow us on Twitter: @TitanBooks

Published by Titan Books, London, in 2019.

Published by arrangement with Blizzard Entertainment, Inc.,
Irvine, California.

A CIP catalogue record for this title is available from the
British Library.

ISBN: 9781789093001

10 9 8 7 6 5 4 3 2

Manufactured in China